"I'm not going to share a bedroom with you again."

Kerry spoke tensely as she continued. "Touch me, I'll disappear into thin air, Alex. I swear it. You can't have me watched all the time."

Long fingers tipped up her chin. "Don't utter foolish threats."

"It's not a foolish threat. It's what will happen," she informed him steadily, her eyes icy-cold. "You've got your son, you've got a wife who will behave like a wife in public. But in private, as far as I'm concerned, the act dies."

"You realize that you are about to turn our marriage into a battle? It won't work, *cara*, I warn you."

She swallowed with difficulty. "Content yourself with what you've got, Alex. It's all you're going to get."

LYNNE GRAHAM was born in Ireland and at the age of fifteen, submitted her first romantic novel to Mills & Boon. Just when she was planning a career, a Christmas visit home resulted in her having to make a choice between career or marriage to a man she had loved since her teens. They live in Ireland in a household overflowing with dogs, plants and books. When their seven-year-old daughter was a toddler, Lynne began writing again, this time with success.

LYNNE GRAHAM

the veranchetti marriage

Harlequin Books

TORONTO • NEW YORK • LONDON
AMSTERDAM • PARIS • SYDNEY • HAMBURG
STOCKHOLM • ATHENS • TOKYO • MILAN

Harlequin Presents first edition May 1989
ISBN 0-373-11167-3

Original hardcover edition published in 1988
by Mills & Boon Limited

CHAPTER ONE

NICKY came hurtling through the crowd ahead of his escort and threw himself into his mother's arms like a miniature whirlwind. 'Missed you,' he confided, burying his dark head under her chin where unmanly tears could be decently concealed.

Kerry's arms encircled him tightly. He had been staying with his father for an entire month. Kerry had watched the calendar through every day of his absence, resenting the unusual silence echoing round the cottage and the emptiness of her weekends. As she slowly lowered her three-year-old son to the ground, she noticed the two dark-suited men lodged several feet away. Nicky's escorts.

One of them stepped forward coolly to say, 'It really wasn't necessary for you to come to the airport, *signora*. We would have brought Nicky home as we usually do.'

There was a studied insolence to the roaming sexual appraisal of his dark eyes. Involuntarily, Kerry's magnolia skin heated. She knew that she shouldn't allow Alex's security staff to browbeat her. But she did. She was nobody of importance on their scale. The discarded ex-wife, who didn't even enjoy a semi-civilised post-divorce relationship with their employer. They could afford to be as rude and superior as they liked. They knew better than anybody that Alex wouldn't even take a phone call from her. The chances of her complaining were negligible.

With a rather valiant effort she lifted her chin. 'I wanted to come to the airport.'

'Mr Veranchetti prefers us to see his son safely to the door of your home, *signora*.'

'I'm perfectly capable of driving my own child home,' she muttered curtly, and turned deliberately away, seeking a fast escape from a confrontation in the centre of Heathrow.

'Until the little boy reaches home he's our responsibility.' A restraining hand actually fell on her tense shoulder.

She couldn't believe this was happening to her. That she was being bullied by a hired security man, who treated her child like Little Lord Fauntleroy. Nicky was her son. He might be Alex's as well, but did she have to stand for such treatment? It was totally destroying Nicky's homecoming. She was aware of her son's brown lustrous gaze fixed anxiously to her strained face, and she strove to behave calmly.

'When I'm here, he's my responsibility,' she stated with a forced smile. 'Really, this is quite ridiculous. All this argument simply because I chose to meet him off the plane . . .'

The other man had stepped forward too. In one hand he carried Nicky's case. A fast exchange of Italian took place over her slightly bowed head. Murderous feelings were struggling for utterance inside her. The past four years had been very tough for Kerry. What she could never accept was that they should continue getting tougher. Alex was zealously trying to wean Nicky from her for longer and longer periods, and she had an absolute wimp of a solicitor, who was always sympathetic but equally trenchant in his view that her ex-husband was not a man to antagonise.

'Mr Veranchetti wouldn't be pleased.' It was the older man who spoke now for the first time.

He talked as if Alex was God. Or maybe the Devil, she conceded abstractedly. People always employed that impressed-to-death tone when they referred to her ex. It had got to the stage where Kerry's blood chilled in her veins whenever he was mentioned. Alex had turned into a remote, untouchable figure of power and incalculable influence long before he had divorced her. It was humiliating to acknowledge that Alex's treatment of her in recent years had left her frankly petrified of him.

But today she suddenly found herself deciding that enough was enough. Nicky was hers and they were—believe it or not—on British soil. She didn't have to stand here being intimidated by Alex's henchmen. There was an angry flash in her copper-lashed green eyes as she stared at both stalwart figures. 'Unfortunately, Mr Veranchetti's wishes don't carry the same weight with me,' she murmured shortly, and stuck out her hand challengingly for her son's case.

After a perceptible hesitation it was handed over. The weight of it almost dislocated her wrist. She was a small woman and slenderly built. But, distinctly uplifted by her minor victory, she released a determined smile.

'Thank you,' she said quietly.

'Why are Enzio and Marco cross?' Nicky hissed up at her in a loud stage-whisper.

'Oh, I'm sure they're not really cross,' she replied cheerfully. 'Give them a wave.'

Nicky turned his curly dark head. 'They're coming after us.'

Well, if they wanted to waste time trailing in her wake

out to the car park, that was their affair. She should have been firmer before now, she told herself bracingly. She shouldn't let strangers' opinions matter to her. But it was her conscience afoot, wasn't it? The fear that they knew why her marriage had broken up. That creepy, crawling and lowering fear that her sordid secret might be common knowledge among the higher echelons of Alex's security staff. It was that which invariably kept her silent: shame. Shame and guilt, even after four long years. *She* no longer felt she was worthy of respect, so she wasn't likely to be granted it by others.

'They're gone,' Nicky said in some disappointment during their long trek to the van.

Kerry's tense shoulders eased a little. She lowered the case and changed it to her other hand. It was a cold, frosty morning, and her ankle-booted feet skidded on the whitened tarmac. She hunched deeper into her electric-blue cord duffle coat and quickened her pace to the blue van parked close to the fence. By the time she had got the case stowed in the rear and had settled in behind the wheel, she was beginning to notice how quiet Nicky was. Normally he was bubbling over with disjointed stories of where he had been, who he had been with and what a fantastic time he had had. For some reason his usual buoyancy was missing.

'Did you have a good time?'

'Oh, yes.' He shot her a rather apprehensive smile as she reversed out of the space.

'So what did you do?' she encouraged.

'We went fishing 'n' swimming . . . and we went up in the jet plane. Nuffin' special,' he muttered, turning his small, serious face away.

No, she guessed it really wasn't anything special to Nicky. From no age at all he had been flying round the globe to rendezvous with his tycoon father. When he had been a baby, Alex had flown to London and a nanny had arrived in a chauffeur-driven car to collect Nicky and ferry him away for the day. But, as Nicky became less dependent on his mother and more familiar with his father, the day trips had gradually become weekends.

He was almost four now, an extremely bright and self-assured little boy. There was no nanny in attendance these days, and a phone call or a letter from Alex's London lawyer heralded arrangements for Nicky's sojourns abroad. Alex had unlimited access to Nicky. When Nicky had been a baby that hadn't bothered her. It had soon become clear that Alex did not intend to encroach too much then. The situation had changed quite rapidly over the past year, as Nicky left the toddler stage behind.

In infuriating addition, Nicky openly adored Alex. She had never been able to fathom that astonishing fact. Alex, so cold, so remote, so capable of sustaining implacable hatred for his child's mother . . . how could he inspire such trust and affection in Nicky? She could not imagine Alex bending to meet a three-year old on his level. But it seemed that he did.

'Mummy, Daddy wants me to live with him.'

Kerry's eyes were in the mirror, dazedly glued to the sight of the silver limousine nosing dexterously in behind the van. Her foot almost hit the brake as Nicky's statement penetrated. 'What did you say?' she whispered sickly. 'Say that again.'

'He asked me if I'd like that,' Nicky volunteered less abruptly.

Kerry let oxygen into her lungs again. What a sneaky, manipulative swine Alex was to ask that of a child Nicky's age! Just a conversation, though. Possibly the sort of conversation she might have had

with Nicky had she been in Alex's shoes—the parent
who got visits rather than round-the-clock privileges. It
didn't mean that she had anything to worry about. After
all, Alex hadn't put up a fight for custody when Nicky
was born. Why should he now?

'What did you tell him?' she prompted carefully.

'Only if you come too. You see, I thought and thought
and thought about it,' Nicky assured her with subdued
Latin melodrama. 'And that's what I'd like the best of
all, an' then I wouldn't have to miss you or Daddy.'

Nicky's solution was touchingly innocent and hair-
raisingly practical. He didn't understand divorce. How
could he? He didn't even understand marriage. He had
yet to see his parents in the same room together.
Mummy and Daddy were entirely dissimilar people,
who lived vastly divergent lives and with whom he did
very different things. Her eyes stung with rueful tears,
and she wished the limousine containing Enzio and
Marco would stop crawling up her bumper. The van did
not go at great speed up hills.

'And what did Daddy say?' she couldn't help
demanding.

'Nothing. He looked cross,' Nicky recalled unhappily.

Cross would have been an understatement, she
envisaged with bitter humour. Was he trying to take
Nicky away from her, or was she being paranoid?

'You still haven't told me what you did in Rome,' she
flipped the subject smoothly. 'Did you go sailing?'

'Helena came too. She's nice. She's got lots of yellow
hair.'

'Oh.' Kerry tried and failed to resist the bait. 'Is she
pretty?'

'Spectacular. Giuseppe says that. Does that mean

pretty?'

She didn't ask who Giuseppe was. Alex had an enormous family of sisters and brothers and nephews and nieces with whom Nicky played when he was abroad. Veranchettis dotted the world. Milan, Rome, Athens, New York. So Alex had another ladyfriend . . . so what?

Alex had had one affair after another since their divorce. Vickie was very good about keeping Kerry up to date. Her sister had once been an international model. Although she had now retired and opened her own modelling agency, she still had a passport into high society circles, and in Europe Alex was pretty hot news. Helena . . . the name didn't ring a bell. She stifled the knifelike pain scything through her. It was bitterness and bile, not jealousy. Jealousy was what you suffered when you loved somebody, and Kerry had stopped loving Alex a long time ago.

She feared him and she hated him in equal parts. He had almost destroyed her. Alex didn't have a forgiving bone in his body. She might as well have beseeched compassion from a granite monolith! Her love had been beaten out of her soul, crushed just as he had crushed her with his distaste and his contempt.

The only good thing to come out of their marriage was Nicky, but she had never doubted that Alex looked on Nicky's conception in a very different light because she was his mother. The fairy-tale marriage had turned into an unmitigated disaster. The dreams had finally turned to ashes, however, in her own clumsy hands. She attempted to dredge herself from her despondent thoughts and listen to Nicky's chatter. He had relaxed now that he had got Alex's question off his chest. He liked his world just the way it was. But would it always be like that?

'Daddy took me to the office and showed me Nonno's picture,' Nicky rattled off importantly.

Kerry grimaced. Dear God, JR had nothing on Alex Start 'em off young. Show him the empire. Show him the desk. She was darned if she wanted Nicky to become an industrialist like Alex. A sort of superior loanshark with a calculator for a brain and a heart which only beat a little faster in the direction of a balance sheet.

'That was nice,' she said diplomatically.

'I'm going to be a fisherman when I grow up, like Giuseppe.'

Not with Alex around, darling. Alex was a lethal mix of Greek and Italian genes, but they all had pedigreed beginnings. His mother had been a Greek shipping heiress, his father the son of an Italian tycoon. It was an explosive mixture, but not on the surface. Outwardly, Alex was twenty-two-carat gold sleek sophistication. Calm, concise, superbly controlled. Sometimes she wondered how she had ever been dumb enough to see other things in Alex. But eighteen-year-olds thought with their hearts and their bodies, not with their heads. They saw what they wanted to see. In her case, that had been a perfect world whose axis centred solely upon Alex. She hadn't seen to either side. She hadn't seen a single flaw. An amount of love which had bordered on obsession had blinded her.

It was starting to snow and she was getting angry about the persistent limousine still purring effortlessly along in her wake. Such nonsense! They had their orders, and like programmed robots they would go to ridiculous lengths to follow Alex's instructions to the last letter. Her shoulders ached with the tension of careful driving, and that monster rolling along on her trail was an added irritant.

It was a lengthy drive to the Hampshire village where she now lived. She owned a half-share in an antiques showroom there. Business had never exactly boomed, but she was within convenient distance of her parents' home. Nicky was very attached to his grandparents. He had strong ties here in England. Alex wouldn't find it that easy to sever those ties, she reflected tautly.

She rounded a twisting corner, still mentally enumerating all the advantages she had over Alex in the parent competition, and there it was. A big black and white cow stuck squarely stationary, dead centre of the road. A soundless scream of horror dammed up in her throat as she spun the wheel in what seemed a hopeless attempt to avoid collision with both the cow and the limousine behind her. On the icy road surface the van slewed into a skid. The hedge and the sky hurtled in a fast blur through the windscreen towards her. Something struck her head and the blackness folded in.

'Nicky!' Kerry surfaced with the scream still in her throat, the cry she had never got to make, except in her own mind. Firm hands pressed her back into the bed and her wild, unbound torrent of curly Titian hair flamed out across the pillow, highlighting the stark pallor of her features. 'Nicky?' she croaked fearfully again.

'Your son is quite safe, Mrs Veranchetti.' The voice was quiet, attached to a calm face beneath a nurse's cap.

The breath rattled in her clogged throat. She raised a hand to cover her aching head, and came in contact with the plaster on her temples. 'He's really all right . . .?'

The nurse deftly straightened the bed. 'He has a few bruises and he did get a fright.'

'Oh, no!' Tears gritted her eyes in a shocked surge. 'I must go to him. where is he?'

'You must stay in bed, Mrs Veranchetti.'

'My name's Taylor, not Veranchetti,' she countered shakily. 'And I want to be with my son.'

The door opened. A tall, spare man in a white coat entered. 'So, you're back with us again, Mrs Veranchetti,' he pronounced with a jovial smile. 'You've been unconscious for a few hours. You had a lucky escape.'

'Mrs Taylor,' the nurse stressed rather drily, making Kerry redden, 'wishes to see her son.'

'Your son's father is with him,' the doctor announced. 'You have nothing to worry about. Everything's under control.'

'F—father . . . Alex?' Kerry gasped incredulously. 'He's here?'

'He arrived two hours ago and your little boy is fine, Mrs . . . er . . . Mrs Taylor.' He quirked a brow at the nurse, as if he was humouring some feminist display, and lifted Kerry's wrist.

Alex was here. Hell, where *was* here? She couldn't be that far from home. How could Alex be here? What time of day was it? Spock would have had a problem beaming up this fast! She sighed. Alex would have been informed immediately of the accident, with his own staff on the scene.

'Calm down, Mrs Taylor. I've told you there's nothing whatsoever to worry about. We intend to keep you in overnight purely for observation.'

'I can't stay in . . . does that mean Nicky's ready to go home?'

'His father said he would take responsibility.'

Something akin to panic assailed Kerry. Would Alex blame her for the accident? No, how could he do that? It wasn't her fault that she had been faced with a straying cow. Or her fault his wretched henchmen had been crawling up her bumper! But Alex, here in the same building . . . her blood ran cold.

'I think a sedative would be a good idea,' the doctor murmured, as if she had suddenly gone deaf.

'I don't want a sedative.' She started to sit up again. 'I'm sorry, but I'm not ill.'

'You're still in shock, Mrs Taylor.'

Ignoring him, she wrenched back the covers. Her head was swimming. She ought to be with Nicky. She stilled. Not if Alex was there, too. She wasn't up to that. After four years, she would sooner face an oncoming train than Alex. Oddly enough, their last meeting had been in a hospital, too, staged hours after Nicky's birth. Her temples pounded with driven tension. Absently, she righted the bedding again in cowardice.

'Please lie down.' The nurse's tone was softly soothing, implying that she was some kind of trying hysteric.

'You won't let him in?' She collapsed back heavily again, the fight drained from her.

'Who?

'My ex-husband.' She shut her eyes. She was both embarrassed and wretched. It wasn't adult. It wasn't normal to be this afraid of a mere meeting. But, nevertheless, fear was a wild creature within her. Nebulous, instinctive, illogical.

'If that's your wish.' The older man met the nurse's eyes. Neither of them saw the point of telling the patient that her ex-husband had already been in for a considerable length of time while she still lay unconscious.

Kerry breathed again, although she was still trembling, wrenched by the knowledge of Nicky's distress and her own absence from his side. A needle pricked her arm and she shuddered in reflex reaction before her lashes slowly dipped.

'She's terrified of him,' the nurse said in an avid undertone. 'Did you notice that? I wonder what . . .?'

'Ours not to reason why, nurse,' he parried drily. 'And Mrs Veranchetti is obviously a very emotional woman.'

The blonde staff nurse continued to study Kerry with overt curiosity. Her narrow-boned and slight body barely made a decent impression on the bed. She looked too youthful to be a divorcee, but the masses of flamboyant and beautiful hair and the delicately pointed face were undeniably stunning. Though Alex Veranchetti was equally worthy of remark, the nurse allowed with a reflective smile.

She had never met a more staggeringly attractive man. Those eyes, she recalled, that delicious growling accent. But she hadn't fancied him quite so much when he stood silently staring down at his ex-wife, not a muscle moving on his face, just staring in a set, uncommonly intent yet unemotional fashion, as if she was nothing whatsoever to do with him. Only when he had enquired if a specialist had been called had she noticed his pallor. But while he had consulted with the doctor he had studiously removed his eyes from the bed, and he had not looked back there again.

It was early evening when Kerry awoke. Light was fading beyond the uncurtained window high up in the wall. Memory came flooding back. Nicky. Alex. She glanced at her watch and found it missing, a patient's plastic identity tag clasped to her wrist in its place. This time she registered that she was in a private room, and she wondered how she would settle the bill.

Steven would be worrying about her, too. Her partner in Antiques Fayre was a furniture restorer. He used the workshop at the rear of the showroom, and by now, although time frequently had no meaning for him, he would be wondering where she was. She had promised to call in on the way home. A drone of voices could be heard beyond the door. She resolved to ask for her clothes. She had to get home, find out about Nicky . . . oh, a dozen things!

As the door opened she sat up, wincing at the renewed throb behind her temples. A light came on, momentarily blinding her before she froze in astonishment, the colour draining from her cheeks.

'I see you are awake,' Alex commented, glossing over her incoherent gasp of shock at his appearance. He shut the door, and for several unbearably tense seconds he simply remained at the foot of the bed, studying her.

Dull-eyed and trembling, she dropped her head. He was etched in her mind's eyes with the utmost clarity. He looked so damnably beautiful. It wasn't the usual word to describe the male of the species, but it was particularly relevant to Alex. He had the dark, perfect features of a fallen angel, and the lean, honed-to-sleekness elegance of a graceful leopard. He was unchanged. He hadn't dropped the remorseless, glittering stare which looked right through her, either.

She could not help but relive their last meeting. 'I have made arrangements for you to return to England with our son,' he had delivered coldly then before leaving her again, impervious to the tears and the agony he must have seen in her face as he destroyed her last hopes of a reconciliation. Her hands clutched together convulsively. Pull yourself together, a little voice warned. He had pulled her apart. She was still a heap of jittery and torn pieces, unlikely ever to achieve wholeness again. To do that, you had to forgive yourself first. You had to like yourself. You had to put the past in its proper place. And Kerry hadn't managed any of that.

The gleaming, amber-gold challenge of his gaze imparted one undeniable message. He hadn't forgotten. She hadn't forgotten, either. How could she forget that she had wrecked their marriage by doing something quite beyond the bounds of forgiveness?

'I am told that you didn't want to see me.' The heavy silence buzzed back into her ears.

It was cat and mouse. Go on, snap me up, Alex. You've done it before, you'll do it again. What's holding you up now? She threaded a nervous hand through the wild tumble of her hair. Accidentally looking up, she caught his magnificent lion-gold eyes following the careless movement of her fingers.

'I hardly thought that you'd want to see me.' She chickened out of a direct attack. She didn't really have the right to condemn. It was that sense of being in the wrong, that enforced acceptance of blame which had almost driven her to the brink of a nervous breakdown when she was pregnant with Nicky.

Alex strolled fluidly over to the window to stare out, presenting his hard-edged profile to her. 'Naturally I wish to discuss the accident with you.'

She shut her eyes on an agonising surge of bitterness. Of course, what else. Four years ago he had refused even to see her to discuss their marriage. He had denied her calls, returned her letters and made it cruelly clear to her that he no longer considered her as his wife. But . . . naturally . . . he could pitch himself up to the contaminated air she breathed now to request an explanation of an accident.

'You find something amusing in this?' Alex shot her a grimly implacable glance.

She went even paler. 'No, there's nothing funny about any of it. It's quite simple really. I went round a corner and there was a cow in the middle of the road. When I tried to avoid it, the van skidded and went sideways, making it virtually impossible for the ... car behind us to avoid hitting us.'

'And this is all you have to say?' Alex prompted.

She had no doubt that he had heard a different story from his security men. A story which showed her in the worst of lights. Perhaps they had implied that she had been driving too fast on icy roads, recklessly endangering Nicky's life.

'Yes, that's all I have to say,' she agreed heavily, pleating the starched white sheet beneath her hand with restless fingers. 'I don't believe I could have avoided the collision.'

'My staff did not mention an animal . . . '

Her control snapped. 'Well, I can assure you that there was one, but I know who you're going to believe, don't I? So it would be a waste of time pleading my own case!' she threw at him bitterly. 'Now, if we can cut the kangaroo court, perhaps you'd tell me how Nicky is.'

Disconcerted by her abrupt loss of temper, his straight ebony brows drew together above his narrowed eyes. 'I will not have you speak to me in such a tone,' he breathed icily.

She hadn't intended to shout, but she found that she didn't feel like apologising. They weren't married now. The past could not permit them to be even distantly polite with each other. Alex had made it that way by shutting her out and communicating with her only through third parties. His unyielding hostility had killed the love she had once had for him. She had accepted the new order. He had no right to subject her to a face-to-face meeting now.

'There's nothing very much that you can do about it, Alex,' she dared. 'I don't jump through hoops when you tell me to any more, I don't . . . '

'Do continue. You're becoming extremely interesting,' he derided softly, but his tone was misleading.

Kerry's voice had trailed away to silence under the smouldering blaze of fury she had ignited in Alex's eyes. Nobody talked to Alex like that. In all probability, nobody ever had. And certainly not the wife he had repudiated. Her fiery head lowered again. What had got into her? If her solicitor had been here, he would have been white to the gills over such reckless provocation.

'I've got nothing more to say,' she muttered through compressed lips.

His gaze rested on her rigidity, then sank to her unsteady hands, and an expression of bleak dissatisfaction tautened his hard bone structure. 'Nicky is with your parents. There was no need for him to remain in hospital.'

'My parents?' Kerry echoed in dismay. 'He's with my parents?'

Alex elevated a brow. 'Did I not say so?'

'But . . . but that means . . . ' She swallowed hard, but her face was full of unconcealed horror. 'You must have gone there as well.'

'Yes, and what a fascinating experience that was.' Alex savoured the admission visibly. 'You never told them the truth, did you? They have no idea why we are divorced. They also appear to be under the illusion that you chose to divorce me.'

Her heartbeat was thudding in her ears. She had no defence against his condemnation, and could only imagine how her parents would have greeted Alex's sudden descent. They would have been polite and they would have been very hospitable. Her father was a retired vicar. Neither of her parents approved of the divorce, or of the fashion in which Nicky was being raised by parents who never even spoke to each other. They had never left Kerry in any doubt that they still regarded Alex as her husband. For better or for worse. Vows taken for a lifetime and not to be discarded at the first hiccup in marital harmony. Stricken nausea churned in her stomach at the idea of Alex and her parents getting within talking distance of each other.

'I couldn't tell them!' she burst out on the peak of a sob which quivered through her tense body. 'It was bad enough when I first came home. The truth would have shattered them.'

'The truth shattered me as well,' he delivered harshly, and turned aside from her. 'But to return to the present . . . had you given me an opportunity to speak earlier, you would have realised that I do not blame you for the accident.'

CHAPTER TWO

SUCH unexpected generosity upon Alex's part shook her. Surprise showed in her strained features, and his hard mouth took on a sardonic curve. 'Nicky gave me his version of the accident. It matched yours. The men concerned will be dismissed,' he revealed flatly.

'For . . . for what?' Kerry whispered, doubly shaken.

'You could both have been killed,' Alex retorted harshly. 'But, apart from that, I will not tolerate lies or half-truths from anyone close to me.'

Or deception, or betrayal. There were no second chances with Alex; Kerry knew that to her cost. In the pool of silence, she was pained by his detachment, the almost chilling politeness which distinguished his attitude. She meant nothing to him, but Nicky did. Nicky was a Veranchetti, and Alex's precious son and heir.

'Your van is, I believe, beyond repair,' he continued with the same devotion to practical matters. 'I will have it replaced.'

She bit her lip. 'That's unnecessary.'

'Allow me to decide what is necessary,' Alex cut in ruthlessly. 'Do you think I do not know how you live? Were it not for my awareness that Nicky goes without nothing that he needs, I would have objected to your independence.'

She said nothing. She was infuriated by his arrogant downgrading of the business she had worked hard to build up. He could keep his wretched money!

She had never wanted it. It was a matter of pride to her that she was self-sufficient. And by being so she had won the cherished anonymity of reverting to her maiden name and finding somewhere to live where she was simply a woman living alone with her child. There were no headlines in Kerry's life now.

'I want to go home tonight,' she told him.

'That would be most foolish.'

She thrust up her chin. 'I have business which happens to be very important to take care of tomorrow.'

'You have a partner.' There was an icy whiplash effect to the reminder. She reminded herself that Alex did not like anyone to argue with him.

'He'll be away tomorrow. In any case, I want to take Nicky home.'

Alex viewed her grimly. 'Nicky is in bed, and perfectly happy to be with his grandparents. Leave him there until you are fit again,' he advised. 'Even to me, it is obvious that you are still in a very emotional state.'

A humourless laugh leapt from her lips. 'And you're surprised?'

He lifted a broad shoulder in an unfeeling shrug. All of a sudden Kerry was on the brink of tears, and she wished that he would leave. So many times she had imagined what she might say to Alex if she ever received the opportunity. Not once had she dreamt that it might turn out to be so harrowing. A barrier the size of the Berlin Wall separated them now. Alex despised her. Alex, she sensed with an inner shudder, still believed that she had got off lightly, without the punishment he would have liked to have dealt her.

'You will be hearing from my lawyers in the near future,' Alex said, consulting the slim, gold watch on his wrist, and she had an insane vision of legal reps leaping out from beneath her bed. 'It's time that Nicky's future is discussed. He will soon be of an age to start school.'

Dumbly she nodded, without noticing the intent appraisal he gave her. 'Yes. I know.'

'I am afraid I have an appointment in London now.' He was looking at the door, and she had the peculiar suspicion that Alex, insensitive or otherwise, was suddenly very eager to be gone. 'I have naturally taken care of the bill here. When you are home again, I will call on you there,' he completed almost abruptly.

Her lashes fluttered dazedly. 'My home? But why?' she demanded apprehensively.

'I will phone before I call,' he responded drily, and then he was gone.

Had he suddenly accepted the need for consultation between them concerning Nicky? Dear God, she preferred his use of third parties now! Fearfully, she wondered what exchanges had taken place between Alex and her parents, and whether something they had said had brought about this surprising change of heart. She shrank from the threat of another distressing session with Alex. It was much too late now for her to be civilised. She didn't want Alex visiting her humble home, invading her cherished privacy and doubtless bringing alive again all those horrible feelings she had become practised at suppressing.

'Well, hi . . . '

Kerry glanced up in astonishment to see her half-sister posing in the doorway, he tall, slender figure enveloped in an oversized fur coat. 'Vickie?'

'No need to look so surprised,' she reproved, strolling in. 'I came home for the weekend. I got the shock of my life when I walked in and found Alex sitting there. When I realised he was calling back here to actually see you, I reckoned you'd need back-up. I've been sitting out in the car park waiting for his car to leave. He didn't stay long, did he?'

Kerry was very relieved to see Vickie. Her sister was the one person alive who could understand what she must be feeling now. Yet, paradoxically, they had never been particularly close. Kerry had barely been thirteen when Vickie left home, keen to escape her frequent clashes with strict parental authority. Since then fences had gradually been mended, but Vickie still remained something of a mystery to Kerry. Cool, offhand, not given to personal confidences and very much a party girl, Vickie had, nevertheless, become Kerry's confidante. But the secrets they shared had still failed to break down Vickie's essential reserve. After a brief phase of greater intimacy during her marriage, Vickie had once more become a rather patronising older sister with whom Kerry had little in common. They invariably met only in their parents' home. But the watery smile curving Kerry's mouth was warmly affectionate.

'No, he didn't stay long. He only wanted to question me about the accident.'

Vickie tossed her pale golden hair, her bright blue eyes pinned piercingly to her younger sister's face. 'And that's all?' she probed tautly. 'He didn't touch on anything else?'

Kerry didn't pretend not to understand her meaning. 'Why should he have? We are divorced,' she sighed. 'But he still loathes me. I could see it in him. The condemnation, the disgust, the . . . '

'Oh, for God's sake, give it a rest!' The interruption

was harsh, exasperated, as Vickie flicked a lighter to the cigarette in her mouth and inhaled deeply. 'Why wind yourself up about it? With Nicky in existence, you were bound to meet sooner or later,' she pointed out, and shrugged. 'You know, I couldn't sit about at home any longer listening to the parents pontificating on the possibility of you and Alex getting back together again. The two of them are so naïve sometimes. Goodness knows what Dad was saying to Alex before I arrived. He's been dying for years to preach at him.'

Guilty colour marked Kerry's complexion as she watched her sister pace restlessly. It must have been very embarrassing for Vickie to walk into such a fraught scenario. After all, she knew the truth behind her sister's broken marriage, and she had loyally kept that secret when she might genuinely have felt it her right to speak up. Kerry swallowed the constriction in her throat. She would never be free of her own conscience, as it was.

'Do you know what was said?' she pressed anxiously. Her father was a warm and kindly man, but her divorce had shocked him to the core. Her refusal to discuss her failed marriage had created a constraint between them which had not lessened over the years.

'Alex didn't drop you in it, obviously.' Vickie made no bones about what Kerry feared. 'They'd have been in need of resuscitation when I got there if he had! Stop fussing, Kerry. Their fond hopes aren't likely to be realised. Do you know why they're not here now? They knew Alex was coming so they decided to stay home. But he'll hardly be visiting again, will he?'

So relieved was she by her sister's assurance that Alex had not reviled her in any way that Kerry barely heard what followed. She slid her feet over the edge of the bed and breathed in. 'Will you give me a lift home?'

'Sure. I brought your handbag and your clothes. They gave them to Alex. I'll go out to the car and collect them. I wasn't sure you would be fit enough to leave.' Vickie eyed her pallor consideringly. 'You don't look too hot.'

'I'll be fine after a night's sleep. Anyway, I've got that American buyer coming tomorrow. I can't afford not to be there for him.'

Vickie made no comment. She had never shown much interest in her sister's business. It was in no way as successful as her own modelling agency. But the dealer, Willard Evans, who regularly bought at Antiques Fayre, was a very important customer to Kerry. It might irritate Steven that Willard probably made a three hundred per cent profit on their finds back home in the States, but Kerry never looked a gift horse in the mouth. Since the building of the new bypass they had considerably less passing trade, and she was equally aware that, talented restorer or not, Steven was no businessman.

They were generally overstocked. Steven bought what he fancied at auctions, rather than what was likely to sell. Without the dealer's visits she believed they would have run into trouble over the poorest months of trading, although she had to admit that their bank manager had always been very reasonable when they had exceeded their overdraft facility.

She thought longingly of home, and wished she could go there, instead of back to the empty cottage. Unfortunately there would be too many questions after Alex's visit. She couldn't face those at a moment when she was wretchedly conscious of the mess she had made of her life. Confession might be good for the soul, but it would create great unhappiness for her parents. She seriously doubted that they would find it possible to forgive her. How could they understand what she could not understand herself?

She had been brought up strictly. Her mother had met John Taylor when she was already well into her thirties. He had been a widower with a three-year-old daughter and a busy parish to maintain. Many had saluted his second marriage as one of extreme good sense. Kerry had never been in any doubt, however, that her parents were quietly devoted to each other. Within a year of their wedding Kerry had been born. Her childhood might reasonably have been described as having been idyllic. Unlike Vickie, she had had few stormy encounters with their parents during the teenage years.

Vickie had left home to become a model. In no time at all her true English rose beauty had ferried her up to the top of the ladder. By the time she was twenty-two, Vickie was a success story, renting a small apartment off Grosvenor Place. The summer that Kerry finished school, Vickie had suggested that Kerry use her apartment while she was abroad.

'It's lying empty, and to tell the truth I'd prefer it occupied,' she had admitted. 'You'll look after my things. Isn't it about time you cut loose from the nest? If you don't watch out, they'll stifle you.'

The Taylors had approved neither of Kerry's delight nor Vickie's generosity. But Kerry had been obstinate in her desire to spend some time in London. She had even managed to find herself a temporary job in a nearby travel agency.

'Just wait until you see the guy who uses the penthouse on the top floor,' Vickie had murmured before she left, giving Kerry the lowdown on her neighbours. 'He's devastating, but I'm never here long enough to make an impression. Anyhow,' she had laughed, 'I guess he's not really my type. He's as conservative as hell. I stuck my neck out once and invited him to a party. He passed, giving me the hint that I shouldn't have asked in the first place. Watch you don't make a lot of noise. He also happens to own this building.'

Kerry had almost sent Alex flying on the day she moved in. She had come rushing full-tilt out of the lift as he was trying to enter it, and they had collided, sending the file in his hand skimming over the floor. With her usual sunny cheer she had scrabbled about picking up scattered papers and chattering about the amount of work he brought home with him. She had received the most glacial smile.

It had had no effect on her at all. She had taken her first proper look at him and her knees had gone wobbly. Devastating, Vickie had said rather scornfully. That combination of black hair and golden eyes had more than devastated Kerry. 'Gosh, you'd make a marvellous portrait study,' she had said crassly, getting abstractedly back into the lift with him.

'I assumed you were going out,' he had drawled flatteningly. 'Do you normally speak to strangers like this?'

'Oh, I'm Kerry Taylor, Vickie's kid sister . . . you must know Vickie. Tall, blonde; she's a model. She lives on the fourth floor.'

'I do not,' he had interposed drily.

She had reddened. 'Well, I'm staying here this summer. I thought you might be wondering who I was. That's why I explained.'

'Your floor,' Alex had slotted into the nervous flood, stopping the lift on the correct level and making it impossible for her to do anything but remove herself.

His unfriendliness had been an unpleasant surprise.
Kerry had been born and brought up in a small
community where she knew everybody. The
anonymity of city life had been a shock to her system.
But in her inimitable way she had made friends
wherever she could. The security men in the foyer
had quickly got on to first-name terms with her as she
flashed in and out, generally late wherever she was
going or rushing back for something she had
forgotten.

Alex had only used his apartment when he was at
his London office. She hadn't known that then. Nor
had she even begun to realise how wealthy he was.
She had seen him regularly, stepping in and out of his
chauffeur-driven car. And the women . . . Vickie had
not warned her about the women.

She came in late one night from a party, and ended
up sharing the lift with Alex and a svelte brunette. It
had hit her that night that she was always looking out
for Alex, and that the days she didn't see him were
distinctly empty ones. Meeting him with the sort of
mature woman she naturally could not compete with
had turned her stomach over sickly. She hadn't been
that naïve. She had known very well that he wasn't
bringing a woman home in the early hours to play
Scrabble. And it had hurt her. She could still
remember standing in that lift, mutinously not
speaking as she usually did, and feeling hatefully,
agonisingly young.

'Goodnight, Kerry,' Alex had murmured silkily,
almost as if he knew what was on her mind.

She hadn't slept that night. She had paced the
lounge, asking herself what kind of baby she was to let
herself become obsessd by a male who didn't know

she was alive.

A week later she had accidentally locked herself out of the apartment. The caretaker had been out, the security guard sympathetic but unable to help beyond offering to force the door for her. In her innocence she had imagined that Alex might have keys and, screwing up her courage, she had gone upstairs. His manservant had only allowed her as far as the hall. Alex had frowned the instant he saw her. 'To what do I owe the honour?' he had demanded drily.

But he had laughed when she muttered about her hope that he had a key. He had asked her if she would like to join him for supper. While she ate he had dredged out her life story and her ambition to study Fine Art at university. His manservant had intervened to announce that the caretaker was now available, and Alex had appraised her disappointed face and said, 'Would you like to dine with me some evening?'

'When?' she had breathed, making no attempt to conceal her delight, and he had laughed again. That was how it had begun.

From the start she had feared that Alex thought she was too immature for him. At thirty, he was already head of the empire his late father had left him. As the eldest in his family he had assumed weighty responsibilities at an early age. In comparison, Kerry had been between school and university, and as carefree and unfailingly cheerful as Alex was serious. It was an attraction of opposites. Her dippy sense of humour and her penchant for disorganisation had fascinated Alex . . . but much against his will.

Their short courtship had been erratic. Alex had tried to keep their relationship cool. Kerry had been wildly and quite frantically in love with him, and probably the whole world including Alex had been painfully conscious of the fact. The one strong card she had had then, without even realising it, was Alex's almost fanatical possessiveness. One afternoon her door had been answered by another man when Alex called unexpectedly.

Roy had been one of Vickie's friends. He had only come to collect stuff that Vickie had let him store in her guest room. Kerry had merely offered him coffee. Alex had misunderstood. By the time that was cleared up, all pretence of playing it cool was over. Alex was laying down the law like Moses off the Mount. Somehow he had started to kiss her, and not as he had indulgently kissed her before. Things had got out of hand and perhaps, knowing Alex, they had done so more by design than accident. He had swept her off to bed in a passionate and stormy mood. Afterwards he had looked down at her and murmured, 'Now you are mine, and damn your age, we're going to get married.'

It had been a breathless, whirlwind romance. Alex had bowled her parents over with his well-bred drawl and cool self-assurance. Kerry had not had a similiar effect upon his family. She had soon appreciated that, behind the polite, cosmopolitan smiles, they all thought Alex was marrying beneath him and, what was more, choosing a female totally untutored in the talents required of a Veranchetti wife.

But, possessed as she had believed herself to be of Alex's love, Kerry had had no doubts. Their beautiful wedding had been followed by a fabulous honeymoon in the West Indies. Alex had then calmly dumped her in Rome with his mother. Athene had disliked Kerry on sight and nothing had given Athene more pleasure than when she was guilty of some social or fashionable gaffe. Within six months, even Kerry's even temper was strained. Confined as she was to an existence of idle ease, it had seemed to her that Alex had only married her to imprison her. He jetted back from abroad, swept her arrogantly off to bed and brushed aside her justifiable complaints with a maddening air of masculine indulgence.

He thought she was too young to run a household of her own. He didn't think she ought to travel with him. All the women in his family had always stayed very properly at home, awaiting their menfolk. The first cracks had come early in their marriage. Lonely, isolated by her poor Italian and family indifference, Kerry had been quietly clambering up the walls when Vickie took a job with a Venetian fashion house.

Against Alex's wishes she had gone to Venice to spend a week with her sister. Alex had flown into Venice and dragged her out of Vickie's apartment as if she was a misbehaving child. She had flatly refused to go home with him. She had not given way. As a result, Alex had labelled Vickie a bad influence.

Amazingly he had, however, agreed to buy them their own house shortly after that episode. They had moved to Florence, and while Alex had grudgingly said that Vickie was welcome to visit, he had not been prepared for Kerry to visit Vickie in Venice again. The crunch had come over Vickie's birthday party. Alex had been in London when she phoned him to ask him to attend the party with her.

She had already been in Venice when she called, which had not precisely soothed Alex's ruffled feathers. 'You realise that if you remain there you are putting our marriage in serious jeopardy,' he had smouldered down the phone. '*Per Dio* I was wrong to marry a headstrong teenager, but do we have to advertise our differences to the world?'

He had also cast several unforgivable remarks on her sister's moral principles. Kerry had come off the phone angry and upset.

'I warned you,' Vickie had drawled ruefully. 'Foreigners are different. Alex would have given you a marvellous affair, but he's no fun at all as a husband. My God, he's locked you up and thrown away the key! He's made you pregnant because he wants to tie you down even more. Don't you see what he's doing to you? He's suffocating you!'

Sooner than cast a wet blanket over Vickie's enjoyment that evening, she had done her best to put up a sparkling front. She remembered little about the later stages of that crowded party. She did recall dancing with an American photographer called Jeff, and he had made her laugh. She must have had too much to drink. The next morning, Vickie had frantically shaken her awake and Jeff had been lying in the bed beside her. A split second later Alex had appeared in the doorway, and if she hadn't been pregnant, she honestly believed that Alex would have killed her there and then in the kind of crime of passion Latin countries understood. Without a single word he had turned on his heel and strode out of the apartment.

Jeff had beat an incredibly fast retreat. Kerry had simply been in shock, horrified to realise that she had gone to bed with another man. Vickie had blamed herself for the whole scenario.

'I didn't give a hoot what you did last night,' she had cried. 'I thought it was time you got to let your hair down, but how could I have known that Alex was going to arrive at seven in the morning and practically force his way in?'

It hadn't been Vickie's fault. In a maudlin, depressed state of mind, Kerry had had to accept that she had fallen into bed with a virtual stranger. It was an unbelievable six months before she set eyes on Alex again. She had returned to their home in Florence to find that he had moved out. Within a week a lawyer arrived and served separation papers on her. It had seemed so important to her then to try and tell Alex that Jeff had not made love to her. A woman knew when she had made love, just as Kerry had known later that day when she calmed down enough to be sensible.

In response she had tried hard to trace Jeff before she left Venice, desperately grasping at the hope that he would tell her exactly what had taken place between them. Unpleasant as she would have found such an embarrassing confrontation, at least she would have had the proper facts. And at the back of her mind had lurked the rather naïve prayer that Jeff might have some mitigating circumstance to proffer, or even some innocent explanation which would turn the entire episode into a storm in a teacup.

But she hadn't even had a surname or an address to work on. Vickie had disclaimed all knowledge of him, confessing that she didn't even know who had brought him to her party, and voicing the opinion that it was a matter best left alone. In her unsuccessful efforts to find him, Kerry had clutched at straws, stubbornly refusing to see the point. That she had been touched at all would be sufficient for Alex. A kiss, a caress, a shameful frolic in the dark . . . it made no difference. It was not the degree of the offence, but the betrayal of trust.

Those months of pregnancy in Florence had been a nightmare. She had stayed indoors all the time, torturing herself hour by hour with guilt, and praying that Alex would eventually relent enough to visit her. He hadn't. His family had left her alone, too. Heaven knew what he had told them. She had finally had to face the fact that Alex had not been satisfied with his marriage before Vickie's party. Why then should he even be prepared to listen to her when she had broken her marital vows?

'We're here. Why are you so damned quiet?' Vickie complained.

Sprung back to the present, Kerry peered out at the gloom of her unlit cottage. Vickie dropped her bag on her lap. 'Thanks,' Kerry sighed. 'Are you going home again?'

'No, I'm driving back to town.' Vickie stared at her with disconcerting anger. 'Honestly, you look practically suicidal. Alex isn't worth any more grief. He was a lousy husband. He was the most selfish, tyrannical, narrow-minded bastard I ever came across. I thought he was about to strangle you that day!'

'Vickie,' she implored wearily.

'You can't still be that sensitive. So you went to bed with another man! Do you think darling Alex spent all those business trips of his sleeping alone? You still have a lot to learn about rich European men,' she condemned cynically.

Sometimes she had wished he *had* killed her that day. Instead he had deprived her of the one thing she could not live without then. Him.

Refusing even a cup of coffee, Vickie drove off. Disappointed by her quick departure, Kerry tiredly unlocked her own front door. Empty. She felt so achingly empty. The cottage was freezing cold. She didn't bother putting on a light. Lifting the phone off the hook in the hall, she passed by into her room and

stripped on the spot before sliding into the icy
unwelcome of the bed. Ever since the divorce she had
kept a strict control on her emotions, and it had
worked. Nothing had ever hurt her since. It hadn't
worked with Alex today. It would have been a
wondrous gift to be frozen and emotion-free with
him.

She fell into a doze around dawn. The doorbell
woke her up. Her drowsy eyes fixed on the alarm
clock, but it had stopped. She crawled out of bed,
shivering in the morning chill. Yanking on her robe,
she hurried to answer the door.

'I did attempt to phone when I realised that you had
left the hospital last night,' Alex drawled sardonically.
'But your phone appears to be lying off the hook.'

'Alex . . . ' Kerry curled back behind the door,
much as if a black mamba had appeared on the step.
Peering round the edge, she said, 'Could . . . could
you come back in an hour?'

'Don't be ridiculous!' His hand firmly thrust the
door wider and he stepped in, flicking an unreadable
glance over her. 'I warned you that you should stay in
hospital.'

Alex could always be depended on to say, I told you
so. She reddened, miserably conscious of being caught
on the hop. He looked sickeningly immaculate in an
expensively tailored dove-grey suit. 'I'll go and get
dressed,' she muttered, and pressed the door of the
lounge open reluctantly. 'You can wait in there.'

After a quick wash she pulled on jeans and a
sweater. When she walked into the lounge he was
standing almost on top of the electric fire with all
three bars burning. She studied his dark, urbane face
and clear, golden eyes from beneath the veil of her
lashes. Tension hummed in the air in a tangible

wave.

Abruptly she dragged her eyes from him. 'Exactly why are you here, Alex?'

CHAPTER THREE

'I WANT to discuss Nicky with you.'

Kerry sank nervously down on to an overstuffed chesterfield and studied Alex's hand-stitched shoes. Icy fingers of dread were clutching at her heart. 'I don't feel so great today,' she muttered apologetically. 'Couldn't we leave this to some other time?'

Alex expelled his breath harshly. 'No, we cannot.'

'My throat's sore.' She edged up shakily again on the limp lie. 'I'm going to make coffee. Do you want one?'

'You're . . . '

She walked out of the room and slid down heavily again on to a chair in the kitchen. Alex was here to tell her that he intended to take Nicky away from her. It would be very like Alex to deliver the death-blow personally. It still astonished her that he had not sought custody when Nicky was born. In an Italian court, as a foreigner with a charge of adultery hanging over her, she would not have had a prayer of retaining her son. Last night she had not let herself think about what he might mean. She had blocked the fear out. But was it likely that Alex would condescend to visit merely to discuss nursery education? Who was she trying to kid?

'I don't want coffee,' Alex said icily from somewhere behind her.

'I don't really care what you want or don't want,' she admitted without even turning her head. 'But you

39

are not getting Nicky. I'll fight you to the death before I'll let you have him.'

'This is scarcely a discussion.'

'Look it up in a dictionary, Alex,' she advised tonelessly. 'You'll discover you have never had one.'

He pulled out a chair opposite and sat down. He looked alien against the backdrop of her homely kitchen. In the pin-drop silence she studied the scarred pine table surface. Alex twice in twenty-four hours was too much to be borne. He should not have come without the prior warning he had promised. Overly conscious of her sleepy, make-up-bare face and jeans, she was mortified. It annoyed her to think that he was probably looking at her now and reflecting that he had had a lucky escape.

'Have you finished?'

She wanted to smash something. The derisive tone bit like acid. 'Just get on with what you came to say,' she prompted thinly. 'I've got to be at the showroom for eleven.

The dark-lashed brilliance of his eyes clashed with hers. She was too angry to try and veil the loathing in her own gaze. His proud bone structure hardened. 'I believe you know what I am here to . . . talk about.'

She went back to scrutinising the table, her slight frame taut as a drawn bow.

'I'm no longer prepared to play so minor a part in my son's life. Once he starts school, how often will I be able to see him?'

Holidays . . . weekends,' she supplied woodenly.

'Apart from the fact that that is insufficient, I happen to live abroad. When he is at school he won't be able to fly hundreds of miles just for a couple of days. It is time that changes were made,' he delivered in the same coolly measured tone. 'Why should I suffer my son to become a stranger to me? It is not my fault that we are divorced. I remind you of that not out of any desire to be unpleasant. I merely state a fact.'

Kerry had gone very pale. Beneath her sweater a trickle of perspiration ran down between her breasts. He knew exactly how and when to insert the knife. Alex considered himself wronged. She was the sinner, but she was most unfairly the guardian of their son.

'What is this man Glenn to you?'

Her Titian head flew back in surprise. 'Steven? What has Steven got to do with this?' she demanded blankly.

Alex lounged back in the chair, perfectly calm, one brown hand resting loosely on the table. He might have been sitting in on a board meeting. 'I asked you a question.'

'Well, you can go sing for the answer! she snapped lunging jerkily out of her chair. Suddenly she saw what Alex was getting at. If he took her to court, he would do whatever he had to do to put up the toughest fight. If that meant smearing her reputation to suggest that she was an unfit mother, he would not retreat from the challenge. When Alex went out to get anything, he put his whole heart in the venture.

Steven was a good friend and her partner. Occasionally he ate here. Sometimes he took her out for a meal when Nicky was away, but those social pairings took place with his girlfriend Barbara's agreement. A nurse with the International Red Cross, Barbara spent very little time in England. They had been in love since they were teenagers, but it was an erratic relationship, spiced by long periods of silence because Steven was reluctant to embrace the responsibility of marriage. He was content as he was, and too lazy to stray when Barbara was unavailable. But why should Kerry explain Steven's love life to Alex? It was none of Alex's business.

A hard hand spun her round. His fingers exerted pressure upon her narrow shoulder-blade. Tawny-gold eyes glittered down at her in a mixture of barely leashed fury and disbelief. In a sense she could sympathise with his incredulity. Four years ago she would not have dared to speak to him like that. But when she looked at the situation as it was, she saw no reason to hide her antipathy and her resentment. Alex would do what he wanted to do, regardless of how she behaved. He had proved that when he had ended their marriage, he had proved it continually in the years since.

'Let go of me!' she ordered, losing confidence as she collided for a heartstopping moment with his hard appraisal. Out of nowhere an odd breathlessness afflicted her, as if his fingers were squeezing her throat instead of her shoulder. 'Alex, if you don't let go of me . . . I'll slap an assault charge on you . . . I've got nothing to lose!'

Dark colour overlaid his bronzed cheekbones, and an unholy flash of naked, seething anger lit his piercing gaze. 'Shall I tell you what I am going to do?' His roughened demand was thickly accented as he stared down at her, releasing his hold upon her with a carelessness which revealed his contempt for her unnecessary threat. 'I am going to do what I should have done when my son was born. Take you back and make you regret the day that you ever dared to forget who you belonged to . . . '

'Kerry backed off against the kitchen cupboard, nervously licking her dry lips. 'What on earth are you talking about?'

Alex cast her a hard, contemptuous smile. With the venting of that aggressive declaration of intent, he appeared to have regained his equilibrium. 'Do you doubt that I can do it? I can't think of why I omitted to do it before. I can have my son in my home. He can even have what he wants. And Nicky wants his mother as well.'

Dazedly she surveyed him. 'But we're divorced.'

'I could marry you again. I'm prepared to do that to get my son. He's still too young to be parted from you,' he murmured shortly.

A brittle, stifled laugh left her lips. 'You're crazy. I wouldn't marry you again if the survival of the human race depended on it!'

A black brow lifted, a ruthless smile slanting his beautiful mouth. 'But what about your survival, Kerry? How would you cope if I told your parents why I divorced you?'

Parchment-pale, her strained features reflected immediate horror. 'Why should you do that? You never see them. It doesn't matter to you what they think . . . '

'Yesterday it stuck in my throat to listen to your father talking about the sanctity of marriage,' he whipped back in silken derision. 'Oh, I know very well what they think. That it was I who strayed into other beds. No doubt you came home and complained at length about the frequency of my trips abroad. They reached their own conclusions. Why did I sit and listen politely in silence to your parents protesting that it is very difficult for our son to be divided between two households? I didn't owe you that silence. I owe you nothing.'

'Alex, I . . . '

He cut across her, 'Last night I reached a decision. I

will have my son and I will have you as well in the same house.'

She was trembling. Even hating him as she did, she could still appreciate that her father's well-meant interference must have dealt a stinging blow to Alex's pride. Alex had nothing to apologise for in terms of marital wrongdoing . . . at least nothing that could be proved and nothing major. His insensitivity towards her needs had not run to verbal or physical abuse. Dear heaven, she marvelled that he had remained silent about the real facts in the face of her father's innocent provocation. What was happening now she didn't really comprehend. It was too immense, too unexpected and too terrifying.

'I presume you understand me.' Alex sent her still figure a fulminating appraisal. 'We will remarry or I will tell your parents what you are too ashamed to tell them. Perhaps it is time they were deprived of their naïve illusions.'

Her lips parted. 'You can't threaten me like that. It's blackmail . . . '

'Why not? If one may be blackmailed by the truth, let it be so.' Alex failed to flinch from her shocked condemnation. 'Why should I be deprived of my son? If I take you to court. I am unlikely to win custody. It is very rare for a mother to lose her child. If I destroy your reputation to achieve my own ends, I not only embarrass my family, I sentence my son to the possession of a mother he can only be ashamed to own to in later years. Mud sticks,' he said succinctly, a fastidious flare to his nostrils. 'I would be no cleaner than you if I began such a battle, and I have more pride in my family name. I will not dishonour it with lurid publicity.'

She realised in stricken apprehension that Alex was

not only coldly serious, he had mulled over the problem in depth. This was not an angry impulse to call her to heel. He wanted Nicky and he was not foolish enough to believe that he could separate his son from his mother without causing him a great deal of pain. In acceptance of the necessity he was prepared to take the two of them.

'Do you realise that my father has a heart condition?' she whispered shakily.

'I didn't know, but that is irrelevant to me. Perhaps you should have thought of that four years ago,' he countered with chill emphasis. 'I have more concern for my son, who is *my* family. To gain him I am prepared to use pressure, and let me assure you, *cara*, if you push me to it, I will carry through the threat. Why should I leave you to bask here in parental love and independence, raising my son as a foreigner in a . . . ' Words appeared to fail Alex as he slashed a scornful glance round her kitchen. His mouth compressed. 'My son should be in my home where he belongs, and he will be there soon if it is the last thing I do.'

Kerry was breathing fast and audibly. Alex had her symbolically up against a brick wall. No matter where she turned, she could see no hope of escape. Until now she had not known the depth of his bitterness. She had his son when she had no right to such a privilege. He had suffered by the loss of Nicky when she was the one in the wrong. She had never even begun to suspect that Alex felt as strongly about the situation. But how could she have? They hadn't talked in all these years, and all this time Alex's indignation had been damming up. Yesterday it had reached new heights in her parents' home, and Kerry had foolishly given him the weapon. She had revealed how afraid she was of them learning the truth.

'You can't do this,' she said weakly again.

Alex vented a humourless laugh. 'Are you going to stop me? If you put your son's needs first, you would not need to be forced. You would see that for him to have two parents and the background to which he was born would be indisputably preferable to what he has now. Shuttled betweeen the two of us like a parcel, confused by two languages, two completely opposing life-styles!' he enumerated in savage repudiation. 'How is he to know who he his?'

She did not need to have Alex throw the drawbacks of their divorce in her face. Did he regret the divorce now? Her soft mouth set cynically. He probably regretted the poor timing of her conception scant weeks before their break-up. Had she not been pregnant, he could have severed their ties for ever and remarried without a backward glance.

'So you have your choice,' he concluded drily.

She bit her lower lip painfully. 'You haven't given me a choice!' she argued furiously.

'You have until tomorrow to give me an answer.' Golden eyes held hers with cruel mockery.

'You ruthless bastard!' she burst out unsteadily.

Lean-fingered hands enclosed her wrists. He jerked her up against his hard, boldly masculine body as if she was a rag doll. 'I'l make you pay for every insult you give me now,' he swore roughly. 'In my bed . . . whenever and however I want you.' Her darkened green eyes widened to their fullest extent. Alex's fingers pushed up her chin, savage amusement burning in his gaze. 'I shall enjoy that. Using you as you used me. I loved you. I loved you beyond the bounds of my own intelligence,' he confessed derisively. 'I was so weak in the grip of that love that I was blind. But I don't love you any more. I don't need you, either.

You have no hold on me now. You don't even have my respect. If I were you, I wouldn't incite my temper any further. You'll only pay for it at a later date.'

The raw emphasis of the assurance left her boneless. His dark-timbred drawl had almost mesmerised her into complete paralysis. But, as his meaning sank in, her stomach somersaulted in violent rejection of his intent. A loud thump which she could hardly recognise as her own heartbeat was pounding in her eardrums.

'*Capisci, cara?*' With a cynical smile, he released her chin. 'Tomorrow afternoon you can present yourself in my office in London. A car will call for you at two. You will leave Nicky with your parents and explain that you are attending a party with me tomorrow evening and staying overnight in London. I doubt if they will place any objection to the plan.'

'Alex . . . you mustn't do this . . . ' she whispered in absolute turmoil. 'I have a life of my own . . . for God's sake, I can't spend the rest of it paying for . . . '

'One mistake?' The golden blaze of his bitterness lanced into her without warning. 'It won't be for the rest of your life. It will be until Nicky is old enough to do without you.'

He left her standing there. He let himself out. She stumbled over to the chair she had earlier forsaken in temper. She hadn't even realised that she was crying. But now her hands covered wet cheeks. She had been wise to fear Alex even when he was invisible in her life, for Alex hated more fiercely than she was capable of hating. He despised her utterly, and he hated her because once he had loved her and she had proved unworthy of that love.

Yet in all those months of their marriage he had not once told her that he loved her. Indeed, it had seemed after the honeymoon was over that Alex was more set upon showing her that he did not need her around constantly. He hadn't devoted much time to her. That primitive and fierce pride of his had seen shame in loving a teenager. Shame and weakness. Perhaps he had believed that it would give her too much power over him if she realised how he really felt about her. Instead he had slotted her into place and shut her out.

She did not doubt the veracity of his declaration of love. By making it, he had twisted something painfully within her. It all seemed such a waste. He had loved her and he hadn't liked loving her. In the end he would have overcome what he saw as a shortcoming. Alex was built that way. It might almost have been a relief when she blotted her copybook and he could rid himself of his despised susceptibility towards her.

But what she was realising now was that Alex had suffered too, and that, in punishing her, he had also been punishing himself. Even if he had relented and come to see her in Florence, though, she was still certain that he would have carried neither pardon nor clemency in his heart. He was hard and inflexible. His standards admitted no adjustments. Wrong was wrong in Alex's eyes.

And in her own. She might have lost her head when he threatened her, but still she saw his reasoning. She could understand his desire to have his son in his own home. She was less able to deal with the ferocity of Alex's desire for revenge. He wanted to make her suffer. He didn't know how much she had already suffered. Understandably, he did not believe that she had ever really loved him. What was she going to do?

Checking the time, she reluctantly put on her coat and set out for the showroom. Fortunately her home was on the outskirts of the village, and Antiques Fayre was on the main street. To her surprise, the showroom was already open. Steven was behind the counter, drinking coffee and chatting to a regular customer, who collected antique plates.

'I thought you had deliveries to make,' Kerry opened ruefully.

He grinned. 'I couldn't be bothered. Have you seen the state of the roads out there? Want some coffee?'

She nodded and watched his slim, golden-haired figure disappear into the back of the shop. Nothing worried Steven—falling trade and irate customers included. On the balance side, he was a non-stop worker with the furniture he loved. His problem was that he restored for personal pleasure rather than profit. In a normal mood she would have chased him out to deliver the completed pieces to the two customers awaiting the return of their furniture. But she was still in shock from Alex's visit.

'He's such a pleasant young man,' the lady plate collector commented, taking her leave. 'He advised me against buying that Spode plate. He's right, it wouldn't really fit my colour scheme.'

Kerry silently gritted her teeth. At present, they couldn't afford helpful advice of that brand. The coffers were far from full. Steven reappeared, clutching a mug. 'So where did you get to yesterday? And what's with the plaster?'

Briefly, she told him about the accident. Immediately, he was concerned. 'You should have stayed in bed today.'

'Willard Evans is coming.'

'Oh, profiteer day, is it?' Steven gathered drily.

'We'd be out of business without him.' She spoke with greater heat than usual, and his blue eyes betrayed surprise. 'Oh, never mind. Can I use your car later? I have to go and pick up Nicky.'

'Do you want me to drive you? You look like death warmed up,' he said wryly. 'Is there something else wrong?'

She pushed her hair off her brow. 'I saw my ex-husband last night,' she confided tightly.

Steven shrugged. 'No big deal, is it? What did he do? Land his private jet on the hospital roof?' He laughed lightly. 'You should have touched him for some alimony, Kerry. I've never understood why you live like you do when you could be sitting in clover.

Her pale skin heated with colour. 'I didn't want to be beholden.'

'Old-fashioned word, that, and not very practical. You've got a kid to think of. Pretty soon he's going to be asking more questions and learning to enjoy his luxury stays with your ex more than he likes coming home.'

'Leave it,' she begged, looking away. 'I'm sorry, I've got a lot on my mind.'

At that point, Willard's hired Mercedes drew up outside. Steven took off, leaving Kerry to deal with him. A small, bespectacled man, he strolled silently though the showroom as usual before making his selections and negotiating prices with her. He never stayed long. He was taciturn for an antiques dealer. He had been coming to them for more than two years, and she didn't believe they had ever exchanged a word of anything that could be deemed personal conversation. It was one of the reasons Steven disliked him.

'There's just something phoney about the guy,' he had said once. 'He never talks. It's just in, out and off for another month.'

'He's very businesslike,' she had argued. 'He doesn't need to make it a social call.'

Today she was grateful for the dealer's undemanding brevity. As soon as he had gone she went out to the rear courtyard and got into Steven's vintage MG. During the drive to her parents' home, she looked back ruefully over the past four years.

She had come home to the vicarage from Florence. She had been shellshocked. Until Alex had walked out of that hospital she had still nurtured desperate hopes of a last-ditch reconciliation. Her parents had been appalled by the news that she was getting a divorce for, over the six months of their separation in Florence, Kerry had continued to write home as if there was nothing wrong. When she did arrive back there had been enough trouble without a confession of infidelity. She had not had the courage to tell them in the state she was in then.

And four months later her father had had a heart attack. Nobody had blamed her, but the shock of her divorce had certainly played its part. It was inconceivable that she now dredge up the murky truth. It was too late and too dangerous. It should have been done four years ago. But would her parents ever have spoken to her again?

Had they turned on her too, she really couldn't have coped at all. As it was, she had been under severe strain. For everybody's sake she had decided to move out and embrace independence. An enormous amount of money had accumulated in her bank account. Alex's money, paid monthly. She could have turned herself into a very merry divorcee. Instead she had withdrawn a comparatively small part of it and bought into a partnership with Steven. She had withdrawn the rest and returned it to Alex's lawyers with the information that she required no further payments. Several letters had followed, trying to persuade her into accepting the allowance. She had stood firm. Living as Alex's dependent was something she could not do, as the guilty partner. Thinking back, she realised that her obstinacy had probably antagonised Alex more, but that had not been her motivation.

The cottage was rented and furnished mostly from the contents of the vicarage attic. Despite her hard work and her appeals to Steven to be more professional, her income had never reached the level she had expected. Steven had needed a partner to stay solvent. He had happily handed over the reins of decision-making to her within the first months. Unfortunately the leopard had not changed his own spots. He still took what money he liked from the takings and lived rent-free in the flat above the shop. In short, Steven quietly went his own way much more comfortably than Kerry ever did.

Her mother was baking when she arrived. The spacious kitchen was full of the aromatic scent of fresh bread. Ellen Taylor had her daughter's build, but her hair was pure white. As Kerry came through the back door, she turned to study her anxiously. 'How are you?'

'I've a slight headache still . . . that's all.' Aware that she sounded stilted, Kerry went on to say, 'Where's Nicky?'

'Out in the greenhouse with your father. Did Alex visit you last night?' Ellen prompted in a tone of eager expectancy.

Kerry nodded and turned away to remove her coat. Here, in this quiet house, her morning confrontation with Alex seemed unreal. She suppressed a shiver. She couldn't tell them the truth. It might kill her father. His rigid moral principles would come into direct opposition with his love for his youngest child. But she had no hope that Alex would withdraw his threat.

Alex was fighting for a worthwile prize. Possession of his son. And Alex was very bitter. Nicky was more important to him than his ex-father-in-law's health. In any case, he blamed Kerry for the whole situation. The original sin had not been his but hers. As far as Alex was concerned, she had got herself into this.

'He came here straight from the hospital. I've never seen Alex so shaken,' her mother confided. 'Of course, you could both have been killed and he realised that. He loves Nicky very much, Kerry.'

Her face set. 'I accept that.'

Her mother cleared her throat awkwardly. 'Nor would I say that he was indifferent to you. Vickie said we were being silly, but sometimes a crisis can bring people together again.'

A day earlier, Kerry would have laughed like a hyena at that suggestion. Alex could have come here and wept crocodile tears had she died. She had the sensation that Alex would not feel that she had paid her dues until she slipped this mortal coil. Her eyelids gritted with moisture. The man she had once loved would not have have employed blackmail tactics. What was she holding off on the glad tidings for? The minute Alex had laid down his demands she had tasted defeat. Alex could yank her back. Alex could do just about anything he wanted to do, because he had her trapped.

'And,' Ellen hesitated, 'he hasn't remarried. He told your father that he didn't believe in divorce . . . '

He believed in the institution fast enough when he had an adulterous wife, she reflected bitterly. But the grim and pointless retort remained unspoken.

'He wants me back.' An edged laugh that was no laugh at all punctuated her abrupt announcement. 'He wants Nicky, and he can't have one of us without the other,' she gibed helplessly.

A pulsating silence had fallen. She glanced up warily. Her mother had stopped listening after the first crucial statement. She looked peculiar, her mouth wide, both brows raised in amazement. 'He wants you back?' she echoed, recovering fast, and she was off in an Olympic sprint to the back door to call, 'John!' down the garden so that her father could share in this wonderful news.

Evidently Ellen could not even imagine Kerry turning any such offer down. In common with Alex, her parents believed that Nicky came first. They had implied more than once that Kerry had walked out on Alex in naïve and selfish haste.

'You did say yes . . . ' Ellen had her handkerchief out now and she was fiddling with it nervously, the unmentionable possibility of refusal belatedly occurring to her.'

'Could you picture Alex allowing me to say no?' Kerry quipped tautly, weighted down by double duplicity.

A beatific smile spread her mother's face and the tears came. 'It'll have to be a register office . . . ' she was lamenting as her husband came through the door.

The die was cast from that moment. John Taylor was not a very worldly man. He gazed at his younger daughter much as if the prodigal had finally made it back to the fold, and the settled down in an armchair by the Aga with an air of dazed and quiet pleasure.

'You were too young at eighteen,' he sighed. 'I warned Alex at the time, but he wouldn't listen. It will be different this time.'

On the brink of hysteria, Kerry stood there, undeniably the spectre at a long-awaited feast, and alone in the trap of fevered and negative emotions. All she could feel was a mixture of fear and fury and disbelief. If somebody had told her yesterday that she would be marrying Alex again, she would have had them committed to protective care. But it really was happening, and all because of a stupid accident. If he hadn't seen her, if he hadn't spoken to her parents, if he hadn't endured the shocked realisation that Nicky might have died yesterday . . . none of this would be happening.

As soon as she could, she escaped. It was very difficult. They wanted her to stay. They wanted details. They seemed to be labouring under the impression that Alex had been so shattered by the sight of her in a hospital bed that he had flung his famed cool to the four winds and demanded that she marry him again because he could not live without her.

'You're doing the right thing,' Ellen declared as she saw her back out to Steven's car. 'Nicky needs the two of you. Everything else will come all right. You'll see.'

She drove off with a sickly smile. The tangled web of deceit seemed only to be getting thicker. She had explained about the party and, as Alex had forecast, they were more than happy to oblige. She hadn't got to take Nicky home at all.

'For goodness' sake, you'll have so much to do,' her mother had protested. 'Packing, sorting out business matters with Steven, getting ready for the party . . . you really ought to go to the hairdresser . . . '

Packing. The word had struck horror into her bones. What was she supposed to do about Steven? He couldn't afford to buy her out. Furthermore, who could tell what might lie ahead? But her logic advised her that, if she left Alex in the future, he would ensure that she did not take Nicky. In other words, marrying Alex a second time would be a one-way ticket, unless he changed his mind.

Steven laughed like a drain when she told him, and then said, 'Fess up, you're pulling my leg, aren't you?'

She sighed, 'No, I'm not.'

'Come on, Kerry. Look at yourself. You don't look like an ex about to happily remarry her ex-husband. You loathe him!' he argued in exasperation. 'What the heck is going on?'

She could not answer his question. What would be the point in dredging it all up? It wouldn't change anything. She assured him that she would remain a silent partner.

He shook his blond head. 'You can't leave me in the lurch. I can't manage without you. Who's going to run the showroom?'

'You'll have to bring someone in. On the other hand,' she suggested gently, 'Barbara once intimated an interest in the business if she could find a niche . . . '

'A niche?' he echoed in dismay, flushing, so that she knew that Barbara had dropped the same hints to him.

'Why not here, when I'm gone? She's a great organiser. I'm sure she could learn the ropes in no time. I did,' Kerry pointed out, ignoring his total absence of enthusiasm.

'We get on better as we are,' he muttered, looking hunted. 'It's more stimulating this way.'

When she finally reached home, she was exhausted. Steven had moaned and groaned until he had outrun her patience. He would have to learn to depend on himself again. Indeed, Kerry's removal from the scene might work to the long-suffering Barbara's advantage. Steven was likely to be very lonely.

She made a sandwich which she nibbled at without great appetite. She tried to phone her sister, but Vickie was out. She kept on trying to picture herself walking cold into Veranchetti Industries tomorrow. Her skin came up goose-flesh at the prospect, and her pride revolted at the humiliation underwritten in surrender.

CHAPTER FOUR

KERRY wished the receptionist would stop staring avidly at her. From the instant she had entered the building she had been aware of the ripple of curious eyes following in her wake. She wondered how many recognised her as Alex's ex-wife. The presence of a security man by her side had raised comment, by granting her a highly misleading air of importance.

'Mrs Veranchetti?' the top-floor receptionist had carolled in surprise. She had looked Kerry up and down, pricing her winter coat and boots, her attention lingering on the luxuriant fall of her hair. She could undoubtedly have accurately enumerated Kerry's freckles by the time Alex got round to seeing her.

His secretary came to show her the way. Alex's office was as she remembered. It was all sunlight and modernity, at glaring odds with the untamed darkness of its inhabitant. He rose from behind his desk, flashing her a brilliant smile. 'Forgive me for keeping you waiting,' he murmured, presumably for his departing secretary's benefit.

Kerry studied him nervously, her colour high. 'Now what?'

He held out an assured brown hand. 'Come here . . . he urged softly.

She stayed where she was, glued to the carpet. A treacherous, relentless awareness of him was quivering through her in response to the burning brush of his lion-gold eyes. Desire and satisfaction mingled there in heady combination. Trembling, she tilted her chin. 'You can force me to come here and you can force me to marry you, but that's all you can force.'

'Is it?' Alex strolled forward fluidly. Long fingers began smoothly to unbutton her coat, then he pushed it down slowly from her shoulders and let the garment drop to the floor.

'Stop it . . . for God's sake, stop it!' she pleaded, for the tension in the air sizzled over her raw nerves.

'Don't challenge me, then.' His hand touched her hair and brushed against her cheek. 'And stop behaving as if you are afraid of me. I don't like it. I've never hurt you.'

Sometimes a physical blow could almost be kinder. She nearly told him that. As he had stripped that coat from her she had had the ridiculous suspicion that he planned to continue with the dress underneath. Now he drew her inexorably closer into the shelter and heat of his tall, powerful body.

'Alex . . . don't,' she implored.

Her slight figure was alternately rigid and shrinking from the torment of his proximity. Something raw and blazing illuminated his narrowed gaze. His dark head bent and he brought his mouth down fiercely upon hers, forcing her soft lips to part for the thrusting invasion of his tongue. It was no gentle or patient reintroduction to his lovemaking. It was shockingly, shatteringly sexual.

His hand settled at the base of her spine, pressing her against his hard, muscled thighs. Heat coursed through her in a debilitating wave. The potency of his masculine arousal was no less overwhelming than the angry hunger of his kiss. A muffled whimper escaped low in her throat. An unbearable, completely unexpected tide of need was wreaking havoc with her sensation starved body. Excitement tore through her in a stormy passage, her mouth opening instinctively for his, her head falling back as his fingers wound into the tangle of her hair. His other hand was wandering at will over her tautening curves, cupping her breast, roaming over the firm swell of her hips in confident reacquaintance. The onslaught seduced her utterly. It had been too long since she had known Alex's touch—indeed, any man's touch. All the heat of desire which had once made her writhe against him in helpless need was controlling her now.

He suddenly loosed her swollen mouth and lifted his dark head. 'I could take you now . . . here, if I wanted.' His fingers slid in derisive retreat from her. 'You have the soul of a wanton, *cara*. It betrays you when you least desire it to. Even with me, whom you profess to hate, you are eager.'

Kerry fell back from him, shaking like a leaf. Her nipples were tight, aching buds beneath her clothes. An ache was spreading within her, an ache she wretchedly acknowledged as a bodily cry for fulfilment. She had never hated herself as she did at that moment for surrendering to Alex when his sole intent had been to demonstrate his contempt. But she'd been woefully unprepared to discover that Alex's lovemaking still drove her crazy, regardless of all common sense. Once Alex had treated her as if she was a precious, fragile creature who might break if roughly handled. What she had lost, what she had destroyed returned to haunt her.

'I have made arrangements.' Thickly lashed golden eyes rested inscrutably on her hot cheeks and evasive gaze. 'We will be married within the week. When you appear in my company tonight we will be announcing to the curious that we are together again. I ordered a selection of clothes to be delivered to the apartment.

You will wear the blue evening gown tonight. I won't be back for dinner, so you'll be dining alone.'

She should have guessed that he would take care of the clothing problem. Her wardrobe no longer contained couture garments. Bitterness assailed her that she should be as helpless in his hands as a child's toy.

'Sit down.' He indicated the chair and lounged back against his tidy desk. 'I have taken a precaution against any future desire you might have to conclude this marriage, too. You will sign a legal, binding contract, agreeing that you give Nicky into my custody if we should part again in the future.'

'You can't ask that of me!' she exclaimed in horror.

'I am not asking, I am demanding,' Alex contradicted with sibilant softness. 'If you conduct yourself as a normal married woman and mother you will have nothing to fear from that contract.'

She searched his harshly set features suspiciously. 'You're planning to do this to take Nicky from me altogether,' she accused. 'You want to make my life so miserable that I'll want to leave.'

His jawline hardened. 'I would not do that to my son. It is natural that there should be storms between us now. But in time those will disappear. If you behave yourself, I have not the smallest intention of making your life a misery,' he parried with a curled lip, as if the very suggestion of such behaviour upon his part was an insult.

'I'll be wretched anyway,' she mumbled, on the brink of angry, cornered tears.

'Why should you be?' Alex demanded in a tone reminiscent of a whiplash. 'You will have a beautiful home, your son, plenty of money, and all for what price? It is I who sacrifices pride in taking you back!'

'How the mighty have fallen . . . '

'*Dio*, don't taunt me!' Alex slashed back savagely but quietly. 'You will sign that contract. You will sell out of your partnership with Glenn. We will make a fresh beginning.'

Had she not had the memory of his loathing for her yesterday, she might have been taken in by this more civilised picture of a reconciliation for Nicky's sake. 'I can't sell out and I won't.'

'We'll talk about that some other time,' he dismissed impatiently.

She took a deep breath. 'Where are you planning for us to live?'

'I have not yet decided.'

'I'm not living with Athene again!' she snapped in dismay.

An expression of icy derision tautened his strong, dark face. 'Why would I take you there to live? You are no longer a teenager.'

Her head bent in comprehension. 'You told her,' she muttered sickly.

'I told no one. But your sister . . . she was not so quiet. There were rumours,' he admitted tautly. 'Unsubstantiated, but damaging.'

She refused to believe that Vickie had talked. But evidently word had somehow got out. Dear God, how humiliating that must have been for Alex! Lion of industry, betrayed by teenage wife.

'Naturally we will have our own home again,' he stressed drily. 'When we first married, I rather innocently believed that you would be happier living with my family and free of the responsibilities of entertaining. I didn't realise that my mother disliked you. It's not always easy to see fault in someone close.'

'I did tell you.'

'Yes, I know you did, but until I witnessed her barely restrained pleasure at the failure of our marriage, I didn't appreciate that you hadn't been exaggerating.'

It was an admission of blame Alex would not have made four years ago, and it mollified her jangling emotions to some degree. She swallowed. 'She . . . your family will be shocked by our remarriage.'

'I am head of my family,' he said with hauteur. 'I will expect you and them to behave with civility and breeding when you meet again. I am answerable to nobody in my private life.'

He bent down, swept up the coat he had stripped from her and extended it to her. 'It's almost five. You will need time to dress for the party.'

She dug her arms stiffly into the sleeves, and was extraordinarily tempted to lean back into the strong, protective heat of him and weep for what she had done in the past and Alex's inability to accept it. 'You know . . . that night . . . ' her tongue slid out to moisten her lips ' . . . Vickie's . . . '

His hands suddenly rested heavily on her tense shoulders.

'That man·. . . we didn't make love,' she whispered jerkily. 'I know that. I don't remember much, but I know that.'

Alex was intimidatingly silent, and then his breath escaped in a hiss. 'It would be wiser if you didn't mention that night again.'

She whirled round. But his embittered eyes made her bite back words of heated disagreement. Either he did not believe her, or she had surmised his feelings correctly. That she had got into the situation at all was sufficient for Alex.

'The car will be waiting for you,' he prompted her departure shortly. 'I will see you later.'

The apartment had barely changed. It was all as she remembered, but for a couple of new paintings and a change of décor in the drawing-room. Umberto, Alex's manservant, might have seen her only the day before. He betrayed neither welcome nor surprise as he politely showed her through to one of the guest-rooms. He opened the wardrobe to display the selection of clothes hanging there. Matching accessories sat on the shelves, and several lingerie boxes reposed untouched on the bed. Alex's efficiency surprised her not at all. For Alex, such gestures were easy. He simply had to lift a phone.

She attempted again to phone her sister, who now lived in a flat in Chiswick which she had bought the previous year. This time, Vickie was home.

'Where the hell are you?' her sister demanded with unexpected shrillness. 'I've been trying to get hold of you for hours!'

'I'm in London, in Alex's apartment.'

'You mean it's true? It can't be, you can't be going back to him!' she argued. 'You've got to be out of your mind after what he did to you!'

Kerry sighed. 'Vickie, I . . . '

'I'll come over.'

'No, don't.' Kerry went on to explain about the party.

'I've got to see you!' Vickie flared. 'You don't understand . . . oh, God . . . ' Her voice trailed away.

Her sister's almost hysterical response to the news that she was returning to Alex surprised Kerry. Vickie very rarely lost control. 'I'll see you tomorrow morning,' she promised. 'Before I go home again.'

Vickie gave a curious laugh. 'OK. I'll stay home for you. Nothing earthshaking is likely to happen between tonight and tomorrow.'

Kerry came off the phone and went to examine the shimmering blue dress which Alex had mentioned. The light caught its glistening, iridescent folds. It was the sort of blatantly alluring gown which Alex would once have frowned upon. Pain snaked within her treacherously. Alex didn't look on her as an innocent any more.

She dined in solitary state. It brought back unwelcome memories of too many other meals eaten alone with one eye to the clock. But this time she was not awaiting Alex with the feverish and resentful impatience of a teenager in love. She was afraid, terrifyingly afraid of the insanity that had taken hold of her in Alex's arms, proving his point that she was ruled by her own physical responses. She had lied to herself all this time in telling herself that she hated him. It was her own self she hated for betraying him. In time, anyone could come to hate the reminder of a wrong. That was what Alex had become to her; an agonising reminder of that night and her own demeaning frailty.

She heard the thud of the front door while she was dressing. The gown was more daring than anything she had ever worn. The swell of her breasts rose seductively above the fitting fabric which hugged from beneath her arms to her hips. The colour was breathtaking against her hair. Picking up the toning bag and the high-collared jacket, she could linger in the bedroom no longer.

Alex entered the drawing-room a few minutes behind her. His eyes swept in rampant appraisal over her. 'Take the jacket off. I want to see you.'

'No. Won't we be late?' she said breathlessly. But she took it off to prevent Alex performing the task for her, and stood there feeling like a slave on the block.

Dark colour had risen to his hard cheekbones. He

made no effort to hide his masculine appreciation.

'You really have grown up.'

The blaze of his sensual scrutiny made her shrug hastily back into the concealment of the jacket. He bit out a soft, grating laugh. 'Surely not so shy? You're almost twenty-four now.'

She was still a case of arrested development. She didn't date. She had never taken another man to her bed. She had spent all this time suppressing an essential part of her womanhood, and presumed that that was why Alex's hand on hers, even briefly, could send a shock of electrifying awareness through her. Frustration. That was all it was, and Alex was tormentingly familiar. She only had to look at him to recall the hard thrust of his all male body on hers, the feel of his satin damp skin beneath her caressing fingertips. Her complexion burnt up hotly, her pulses quickening. In bed there had never been distance between them. But there had been several women in Alex's arms since she had last rested there. Accepting that cruel reality cooled her fluttering senses.

Despite the divorce, Kerry had never learnt to stop thinking of Alex as her husband. He had taken his revenge in full the first time she lifted a newspaper and saw a photo of him in a New York nightclub with a glamorous socialite clinging to him. She had been sick with jealousy, but she had not been entitled to the emotion. They had been divorced by then.

The party was a glittering crush which contained not a single familiar face. Alex kept one arm round her the whole time. They were the centre of attention, and Alex seemed content to be on display. When a well-known gossip columnist appoached them, he smilingly announced their marital plans.

'What have you been doing since your divorce?' she

asked Kerry bluntly. 'You disappeared right off the social scene.'

Kerry tipped more champagene down her dry throat, an ignominious desire to giggle attacking her as Alex smoothly stepped in to speak for her, as he had done on several other occasions throughout the evening.

'My wife was living in the country.'

'Selling plates,' Kerry added brightly. 'Atoning for my . . . . ' She collided involuntarily with Alex's dark eyes, and inwardly she collapsed like a pricked balloon. He made some witty remark, smoothing over her crazy outburst, and she studied the carpet, feeling like a child about to be put in the corner. Really, an ex-wife who had painted the town red would have been an intolerable threat to Alex's idea of what was decent. Without even trying, she had done what would have pleased most, she acknowledged bitterly. She had lived like a nun.

'Don't ever do that again,' Alex growled as the woman moved away. 'And don't drink any more. You've had enough. I'm surprised you can even touch alcohol after . . . '

A chill ran over her flesh and doused the rebellion incited by an entire evening spent firmly beneath Alex's thumb.

His chiselled mouth compressed. 'I should not have said that,' he drawled curtly. 'I apologise.'

It was an apology of glacial and grudging proportions. Ahead of her stretched a lifetime of them. Her infidelity was as fresh as yesterday to Alex, and it always would be.

'You're never going to trust me again, are you?' she muttered sickly.

'I wouldn't trust you to the foot of the street,' he

agreed in a simmering undertone. 'And it gives me no pleasure to tell you that. But since I believe that you are . . . genuinely sorry . . . '

'You mean, you really believe that?' Shame could not drown out anger. 'You'd have been much happier if I put myself over a cliff somewhere, Alex. That's your idea of genuinely sorry,' she whispered strickenly. 'And you damned near succeeded in getting your wish. If I hadn't been pregancant I . . . I . . . '

He had lost colour. 'Don't talk like that!' he snapped.

'No, you don't want to hear it, do you? All about the revenge you took then.' Her tremulous voice was breaking. 'How you let me crawl . . . I'll never forget that, Alex, and I'll never . . . forgive you either . . . '

He swept her out to the hall and sent a maid off for her jacket while smoothly thanking their hostess for her hospitality. She noticed the columnist covertly absorbing their departure and she reddened miserably, regretting her loss of control. But she could not for ever hang her head in remorseful silence, listening to Alex bestow pious comments. She was only human. The trouble was that Alex wasn't. Even loving her, he had given no quarter to either of them. He had meted out punishment with a ruthlessness which still had the power to make her shiver.

'You will never forgive me . . . ha!' Alex vented in the suffocating atmosphere in the rear of the limousine. 'You wrecked our marriage. You went out like a spoilt, over-indulged brat and got drunk and gave yourself to another man while you carried my child. Am I to apologise for not having it within me to forgive you? I knew I couldn't. I stayed away for your safety, too. You were pregnant, you might have lost the baby. Perhaps I was hard upon you . . . '

Her teeth had bitten into her tongue, and the salty tang of blood had filtered into her mouth. 'There is no perhaps about it. You nearly destroyed me. I loved you.'

'If you had loved me, you would never have let another man touch you, drunk or sober!' Alex ripped back at her, all cool abandoned now that they were in private. 'Do not talk of love to me. You were infatuated. Once the novelty had worn off, you wanted your freedom back.'

'That's untrue . . . I was unhappy, but I didn't regret marrying you.'

'Well, believe me,' Alex breathed cruelly, 'I regretted marrying you.'

Dear God, what sort of relationship were they to have in the future? Alex tearing at her continually for a past she could not wipe out, and Kerry hating him for the grain of truth in every pronouncement. It was a vicious circle.

He sighed. 'I don't wish to talk to you like this. I concede that I made mistakes too. Instead of giving way to my desire for you, I should have decided upon a long engagement, during which we could both have adapted to the differences between us. You were too young and insecure, and I was too selfish and intolerant,' he conceded tautly. 'I should have bought us a home in England. You would have had your own family then, and I would not have felt the need to play both father and lover. The combination does not work, and I disliked the necessity, but I asked for the problem.'

His generosity surprised her afresh. There had been a time when Alex could not have admitted being less than perfect. But he had looked back, he had seen the distance which had forged them apart. 'I did love you.' She didn't know why it was so important that he accept that now, but it was.

Alex shot her a caustic and cynical smile. 'For the last time, I do not want to hear you talk about love. It got us nowhere in the past. If it was love, it was a shallow and mawkish sentiment. All I want from you now is the outward show of wife and mother. That should not tax your ingenuity too much.'

Deeply hurt, she turned her head aside.

'Do you want a nightcap?' he asked as they entered the apartment.

She shook her head. 'I'll go to my room,' she muttered tightly. 'As they say, the show's over.'

'On the contrary . . . ' Black-lashed golden eyes met hers in glancing challenge. 'It's only beginning.'

Kerry retreated to her room and twisted angrily out of the dress. She thrust it from her sight bitterly. Alex had dressed her as he saw her now. As a woman on offer to the highest bidder. A woman who could respond to his caresses as happily as she could respond to any other attractive man's. A woman who was easy sexually. Easy to seduce, easy to take. Dear God, that wasn't her! 'That isn't me,' she muttered in soundless despair to the mirror. If she had been like that there would have been a lot of other men since their divorce.

To think of Alex possessing her again with contempt and a hard desire to humiliate turned her stomach over queasily. She couldn't let that happen. She could go back to him, live with him, take whatever he had to throw at her, but she could not let him use her body. Whatever she had done, she was still an individual with a right to self-determination.

She slipped into bed and lay there. Alex was no

rapist. He wouldn't force her to accede to his sexual demands. How could he really even want her? If she made it clear how she felt . . . oh, dear lord, Alex was the most Latin of men in that field. Even if he didn't desire her, he would go through the roof if she tried to bar him from her bedroom. She would have to be more subtle than that.

The door opened and she pulled herself up against the banked-up pillows, huge green eyes wide in the lamplight. Alex shut the door again with a decisive snap. He wore only a short black robe. A tangled mat of dark hairs showed between the parted edges. 'Why should I wait for what I want?' he drawled softly, unperturbed by her obvious shock at his appearance.

'You can't . . . we're not married!' Wildly disconcerted by his unashamed intent, Kerry studied him in shaken disbelief.

Alex padded calmly over to the side of the bed, his long fingers already lazily loosening the tie of the robe. 'We will be,' he parried.

'Th . . . that's not the point! I don't want this!' she hurled at him wrathfully. 'You can't do this!'

He shed the robe fluidly. ' "Can't" doesn't belong in my vocabulary, just as 'no' does not belong in yours.' Dark golden eyes held hers in fierce and obdurate purpose. 'When I have made your body mine again, I will have obliterated other memories with my own. *Capisci, cara?'*

In Alex, twentieth-century female liberation had only ever received lip-service. Not an inch beneath the surface ran the hot-blooded buccaneering instincts of his seagoing forebears and the dark, domineering strength of a man who had absolute conviction in his own innate superiority over the female sex. It was the ice on the outside and the tantalising hint of the fire underneath which had first drawn her to Alex.

Dry-mouthed, in paralysis, she took in his lean, sun-darkened nudity. There was nothing shy about Alex in the bedroom. But Kerry had always possessed a girlish modesty which had in the past amused him. Something told her that there would be no such allowances made tonight.

'You can't,' she whispered. 'It would be wrong.'

'Wrong?' He wrenched back the duvet and got in beside her with a harsh laugh. Her skin burned hot and tight over her bones as he gathered her into his arms, making no attempt to conceal his obvious arousal from her. 'No, this is not wrong,' he asserted arrogantly. 'I will not be easy until I have known you again in the only fashion in which I ever knew you.'

Rage shuddering through her, she endeavoured to evade his hold. He had planned this all along, and in her innocence she had trustingly agreed to spend the night, never suspecting the depths of Alex's determination to mortify what little self-respect she had left. 'No!' she raked at him.

His hand closed on the bodice of her cotton nightdress and ripped it asunder. It was a gesture not of violence, but of sheer cool resolution. 'Either submit or leave,' he challenged her ruthlessly. 'I gave you the terms before you came to me today, and you are still free to change your mind.'

Her shaking hands drew together the remnants of the destroyed garment. She turned the pale curve of her cheek aside in anguish and despair. He had changed, and it wasn't only love that he had lost in the intervening years. He appeared devoid of tenderness and compassion, too.

'And you'll be content with submission, will you?' she muttered tremulously. 'Knowing that you are humiliating me, knowing that I have no choice?'

'Yes, I will be content,' he grated, his golden gaze skimming stormily to the revealed upper curves of her breasts. 'I want you. God forgive me for it, but I want you on any terms, and I do not need you to preach on the subject of my fastidiousness. I am damned if I will deny myself what you could give to a stranger.'

She shrank under the duvet with pained remembrance of what had rent both their lives asunder. He would enforce his mastery in this relationship. He would take her to prove that he was no longer sensitive to her infidelity. But in doing so, she swore, he would receive little satisfaction.

'Put the light out,' she mumbled.

'No . . . do you know how many women have turned into you in the dark over the years?' His savagery flailed her. 'But you are no longer special to me. I will satisfy myself in that tonight.'

'I'll hate you for this until the day I die!' she hissed. 'You're barbaric!'

'You made me that way.' His powerful body was blocking out the light, shadowing her hectically flushed face. 'Why shouldn't you taste the fruits of your own endeavours?' he demanded with seething bitterness. 'But I will give you pleasure, even if it is only an empty pleasure. It ought to satisfy you. I wonder how many other men there have been to give you that same pleasure . . . '

'None; you turned me off men for life!'

His sensual mouth twisted. 'I cannot believe that.'

'I don't care what you believe, you savage!' she snapped back, outraged beyond all bearing by his insults.

The force of his mouth drove her head back against the pillows. The power of his hunger ravaged her. She

lay completely still, a peculiar weakness overwhelming her. He would not use his superior strength
against her. She was in no danger of a forced
possession. Yet, even knowing that a struggle would
drive him from her in aversion, she did not move a
muscle. And even in the instant of questioning the
inconsistency of her behaviour, a shaft of arrowing
excitement seized her and drove her mind blank, as
his hand moved expertly against her breast, brushing
aside the ripped cotton, curving to the unbearably
sensitive mound beneath. He muttered something
thick and impossibly sexy in Italian, and she
shuddered against the tautened length of his body.

I mustn't, I mustn't, I mustn't was rhyming in her
subconscious, in a litany already becoming meaningless. His fingertips found the engorged bud of her
nipple and he lowered his mouth there, employing his
tongue and the edge of his teeth in a grazing,
tormenting caress, while his other hand prepared the
neglected twin for a similar onslaught. Her defence
system flew down like a domino run. Her back
arched. The blood was pounding in insane excitement
through her veins, and the pleasure was breath-
takingly all-encompassing. It had never been so
intense or so powerful for her. Her fluttering fingers
tangled with the blackness of his thick hair, and she
was lost beyond reclaim in a physical world of
sensation. A pervasive heat was building up
agonisingly inside her. Her thighs parted at the brush
of his fingertips.

'You want me . . . badly,' Alex muttered roughly,
his eyes brilliant with triumph. 'Very badly.'

She could not have denied him. Need was a
burning, remorseless compulsion within her
traitorous body, a dam-burst of hunger ignited by his

first touch. As he explored her intimately, he captured her swollen lips again in an urgent admission of impatience. His weight came down on her as he slid between her legs and he took her in a sudden, passionate storm. There was a moment of unforewarned discomfort, followed by the torment of a passion rising close to assuagement. He thrust into her powerfully, conquering her brief spasm of withdrawal, and suddenly she was clinging to him in the grip of an ecstasy which was intolerable. It finally pushed her over the edge, and Alex jerked against her with a surging groan of satisfaction, driving his body violently into the pliancy of hers.

As the clouds of passion receded, Kerry was devastated by what she had willingly surrendered. She had never lost control with such utter completeness. Nor had Alex ever made love to her in a combination of savage passion and volcanic impatience. Desolation and shame over her own abandonment swept her in the aftermath of the empty pleasure he had promised. To have given herself unstintingly to a male who reviled her was surely the lowest level a woman could sink to. Tears clogged her lashes.

'You still belong to me,' Alex murmured unfeelingly.

'You swine . . . I hope you're satisfied!' she said shakily, wrenching free of his relaxed body.

The light went out at the touch of his hand. 'I haven't begun to be satisfied, *cara*,' he contradicted silkily. He ran a taunting hand down over the naked curve of her spine. 'That was for necessity . . . an exorcism, if you like. This time it will be for enjoyment.'

'Don't make me hate you.' Her whisper was choked.

'Hatred can be so refreshing,' Alex fielded lazily, and reached for her again. 'And you have an endless capacity for enjoyment. Why not accept the inevitable? I only ever play to win, and you're in the loser's corner. We know the worst of each other. At least there won't be any unpleasant surprises in the future.'

His lips tasted hers. She was too weak and too shaken to resist. A tiny part of her seemed to think she deserved this treatment, just as Alex believed she had deserved it. She squeezed her eyes shut in the darkness. Within seconds delight and more delight, and the curious reflection that this was, after all, Alex, had intermingled, and she gave herself up to the ecstasy again.

CHAPTER FIVE

'SATURDAY.' Alex delivered the wedding date with careless cool. 'A car will pick you up from your parents' home at ten. I'll contact them today and invite them to join us.'

Kerry mutely watched him embark on his third cup of coffee. Alex had eaten a very hearty breakfast. But he didn't have the demeanour of a condemned man. He was in an extremely good mood, dark golden eyes resting on her at least once every minute with veiled satisfaction. She was in torment. She didn't care that he had no plans to repeat last night before the wedding. It was too late to find comfort in the news.

Alex had achieved exactly what he wanted to achieve. He had subdued her. Her response had made a nonsense of claims of hatred and undying hostility. She felt as if she had been plundered by a Viking attack force. He had taken her in lust and revenge, and he had destroyed indefinably precious memories of the past. His act of exorcism had cost her too dearly.

'One of my accountants will sort out your business investment.'

'No, they won't!' she picked up hurriedly. 'Steven couldn't afford to buy me out.'

Alex moved a nebulously expressive hand. 'His problem,' he said succinctly. 'Throughout your association, he took gross advantage of you.'

'What are you talking about? How would you know?'

'I have maintained an interest in your affairs, and that has not been to your disadvantage,' he emphasised unsmilingly.

She tilted her chin, her eyes blank. 'Meaning?'

'You really want to know?' Alex gave a shrug of almost rueful acceptance. 'You could well have been out of business by now, were it not for certain measures I took. I informed your bank manager in confidence that I would guarantee any debts or loans.'

Horrified, she stared at him. 'How could you?' she whispered.

He sighed. 'You haven't suffered by his understanding when you have been in difficulties.'

'That's not the point. How dare you go behind my back?' she flared, her pride stung beyond measure. She had worked so hard at independence, and all the time Alex had been in the background, propping her up.

'Evans was also under my instructions.' At her second arrested gasp, colour darkened his features. 'I tell you this because deception is abhorrent to me, but you gave me little choice when you refused to let me keep you.'

She was choking on a sensation of drowning now. Willard, too . . . she should have guessed the dealer was too good to be true. Always willing to buy, never failing to turn up, month after month. A paid employee of Alex's sent in to keep Antiques Fayre afloat. 'How could you?' she said again helplessly.

His eyes were wry. 'You are handicapped by your partner's deficiencies, not your own. You worked for him as if you were an employee.'

'That isn't true. I ran the business!'

'Then why does he appear to benefit much more richly than you from the profits?' enquired Alex drily.

'I thought you were having an affair with him. I could see no other reason for such generosity upon your part.'

She hated him for speaking cold, hard facts. She had never got over the feeling that Antiques Fayre was really Steven's. He had started the business up. She had been further restricted by his genuinely pleasant nature. Irresponsible and extravagant Steven might be, but should she ever be in trouble, she could find no better friend. Even so, she should have overcome her embarrassment a long time ago and insisted that Steven draw a wage and no more from the showroom.

'Kerry, had you not been hampered by your partner, I believe your business would have thrived. You shouldn't blame yourself.'

'I'm not blaming myself!' It was the last straw to have Alex, from the pinnacle of his millions, soothing her wounded pride. 'I'm blaming you for interfering in my life and treating me like a helpless child! If I had ever needed help I would have written to your lawyers.'

'From your ditch?' Alex enquired sardonically. 'We both know you would have sooner elected to starve than accept assistance from me. It was simplest to ensure that you managed with a little discreet help.'

'Thank you for nothing!' She stalked out of the room.

He had taken everything now. Furthermore, it was obvious that Alex had kept her under close surveillance since their divorce. He had been spying on her. No wonder he had suspected Steven was her lover. There had been no other evidence of a man in her life. Last night he had learnt differently. He had it all now, right down to the ego-boosting discovery that she had spent four celibate years doing penance for her sins.

'Don't walk away from me, *cara*.' His hand pulled her firmly round. "I did nothing wrong. I was responsible for you and Nicky. Had I been less generous, I could have decreed that you lived a very different life. I could have forced you to be dependent by demanding that you give my son a more suitable backdrop. I let you go your own way while Nicky was still a baby, but you have gone that road to its end now.'

'Don't you dare come that prophet-of-doom stuff on me again!' she warned wrathfully. 'I'm not one of the family yes-women you're used to. I've got brains and I've got just as much need for a life outside the home as you have! Do you hear me, Alex?'

'I should imagine the whole block can hear you,' he said drily.

'Well, you were the one who taught me that a higher octave is the only way that you stop and listen! I nearly died of boredom the last time we were married . . . '

'Not in the bedroom . . . '

'You see?' she interrupted in a burst of anger. 'You wouldn't talk to a man like that. You wouldn't humiliate a man by telling him that you had been bolstering up his business, either!'

He caught her fingers tightly. 'I told you because I wanted no more secrets between us, not because I wanted to belittle your achievements. Can't you be grateful for the feeling behind the interference?'

'I've got nothing to be grateful for after last night. You can stamp the account paid in full,' she retorted bitterly.

'You wanted me.'

'Not in cold blood,' she muttered in deep chagrin.

'Any respect I had for you died last night. Oh, don't
tell me you didn't force me. You just pushed me to the
edge and said jump. There's very little difference.'

She spun away into the bedroom. He had not been
with her when she awoke. Strangely enough, that
circumstance had added to her sense of having been
demeaned beyond the bounds of acceptance. She was
in tumultuous conflict with herself. Yes, she had
wanted him, madly, desperately. In the light of the
day, the heated passage of the night only made her
cringe. She had once expressed love sharing Alex's
bed. What had she been doing last night? Submitting
with pleasure? Reliving the past? Seeking redemption
for her sins? Whatever she had believed she was
doing, she had humiliated herself.

All through breakfast she had hardly been able to
take her eyes off him. Habit was there, a terrible
dangerous familiarity was there. But Alex was not the
same man he had been four years ago. At one stage she
could actually remember pretending to herself that he
still cared about her. How pathetic could you get?
While she had been pitifully deluding herself, Alex
had been making her beg for his final possession. Alex
had brought his bitterness into the bedroom, and her
own wantonness had sunk her beneath reproach.

In less than four crazy days Alex had turned her
inside out. She didn't know herself any more. Or
perhaps she was afraid to probe too deep. Perhaps she
preferred to believe that physical desire alone had
betrayed her. Behind that lurked a bigger
apprehension. She stared strickenly at her overbright
eyes in the mirror. Suppose some of that old love still
lingered . . .? Oh, lord, she mustn't even think this
way. Alex would never love her again. To love him
would be to sign her own death warrant, the final seal

on his revenge.

A knock sounded on the door. She knew it was Alex. The knock was a positive joke after the fashion in which he had entered this same room last night. He was framed by the doorway, dark and devilishly controlled. 'We can't continue to fight like this. It won't benefit our son to see us clawing at each other.'

'Did you think of that last night?'

The golden eyes glinted. 'Am I to hear of that for ever? We are not children. We were married once. In a few days' time we will be married again.'

'You took advantage.'

'I wanted you and I had the right,' Alex stated with unequivocable arrogance.

She bent her head. 'You didn't. We're divorced.'

'I have never felt divorced, I have never felt truly free!' Alex sizzled back in a condemnation that suggested it was her fault. 'I did not think of us as divorced from the moment I saw you again.'

It made little difference to Kerry's feelings. As her hands laced tightly together, another fear occurred to her, and she went pale and then pink. She couldn't bear it if he had made her pregnant. It was no melodramatic fear. Her previous pregnancy she recalled as a ghastly ordeal. Once she had lost Alex she had had no pleasure from her condition. She had been sick almost continuously, and more depressed than any woman ought to be. Bitterly, miserably, she threw him a glance. 'If last night has any . . . repercussions, I'm not having it. I'm telling you that now. I will never go through what I went through again . . . not for you . . . not for anybody,' she swore.

Stark pallor slowly stretched beneath his golden skin. His facial muscles tautened. She assumed that he had not even thought along such mundane lines. A male bent on slaking his lust did not think of consequences.

'Then we must hope that there will be no repercussions,' he replied harshly. 'I don't expect you to undergo something you found so objectionable a second time. Now, the lawyer will be arriving soon with the contract I mentioned. When it is signed, the car will take you home.'

She had the weirdest suspicion that she had cut Alex to the bone. Dazedly, she squashed the idea. He had his son. He didn't need any more children. Nor could he want another tie to her when he had already made it clear that he did not expect them to remain together indefinitely.

The lawyer was elderly. He opened his mouth to explain the thick document to her. Alex cut him off after one word. 'Just slash an X where we have to sign,' he instructed drily. 'I have naturally explained the meaning of the contract to my wife.'

'But as an interested party . . .' The older man flushed, probably thinking on the danger of offending so wealthy a client. He dutifully penned in the X. They signed. Alex then beamed with positive benevolence upon him. Kerry presumed that the contract tied her up in knots. Why else would Alex smile?

Umberto packed her new clothes. She put on a fine turquoise wool suit with a high-necked white silk blouse. Once more she was Kerry Veranchetti. Kerry Taylor had vanished. If Alex had chosen the clothes, he had fantastic taste. Her own had not been half so elegant in the past. She had pursued fashion with teenage extremity. Her avant-garde appearance must have embarrassed him at least once, but a word of criticism had never passed his lips. With hindsight, she marvelled at his restraint.

*   *   *

Vickie swung open her door and simply stared. Her eyes roamed in astonishment over the designer suit. 'What was that I said about nothing untoward happening between last night and today?' she gibed with a contemptuously curled lip. 'Funny, I did think you had more pride. Alex develops some crazy notion to marry you again, and already you're trotting about in fancy feathers. Anybody would think you can't wait to get back there!'

Kerry reddened as she followed her tall sister into the lounge. 'I did try to phone you before I came to London.'

'What happened?'

Kerry chewed her lower lip. When it came to the point, she couldn't tell Vickie everything. Somehow she felt that that would be stabbing Alex in the back. He had employed blackmail because he was desperate to gain custody of his son. And last night? She was equally to blame. She hadn't screamed the place down, had she? She hadn't thrown a chair through his triple glazing and threatened to embrace death before dishonour either, had she? No, far from it. Only afterwards had she had the decency to regret her behaviour.

'Why the beetroot-red blush?' Vickie straightened, slinging her lighter down and blowing a faint smoke-ring as she exhaled. 'Did he use sex?' My God, he must have been desperate to get you any way he could!'

The high-pitched, venomous tone grated on Kerry's nerves. 'It was I who broke the marriage up,' she said defensively.

'And you're going back out of guilt? Alex wants Nicky,' Vickie guessed shrewdly. 'You don't still love him, surely?'

'Of course I don't.'

'He's about as lovable as a sabre-toothed tiger, and

about as dated.' Her laugh was harsh, her blue eyes intent on Kerry's perplexed face. 'Well, I can release you from the weight of your conscience. Would you like a drink?'

'Too early for me.' She was uncomfortable with the strangeness of her sister's mood. In her opinion Vickie had already had a couple of drinks.

Vickie jerked a slim shoulder. 'You might change your mind in a minute or two. The . . . the night of the party . . . or maybe I ought to begin before that.' Her strained gaze was oddly pleading. 'I hope that you remember that I didn't have to tell you this.'

'Tell me what?'

Vickie took a deep breath. 'When we were younger, I used to resent you . . . '

'Me?' Kerry gaped.

Vickie sighed ruefully. 'You were always the favourite at home. You worked hard at school, steered clear of too many different boyfriends . . . you never put a foot wrong. Of course I resented you. But after I'd been away for a few years I felt bad about it. That's why I let you have my flat that summer. I was ready to play big sister.'

Kerry was completely motionless. She had often wistfully envied Vickie her glamour, her poise and her classic beauty. But Vickie wasn't confessing to simple envy. Vickie, she sensed, was talking about sincere and bitter dislike.

'I can hardly believe you never guessed. The parents certainly did. You see, I wanted Alex for myself.' There was a crack in Vickie's stark and shattering admission. 'I cast out every lure there was for him. I invited him to my parties and he never came. Every time he saw me, he acted like he didn't know me. And then you moved into my apartment, and in two months, my eighteen-year-old sister in her ragbag clothes had his ring on her finger, and my God, but I hated you for that!'

Chalk-white now, Kerry's face was filled with dawning horror. 'You were in love with Alex?'

'No, not in love. But he was the man I had set my sights on.' Vickie's voice wobbled, at odds with her shuttered expression. 'I never got close enough to get thinking about love, but believe me, I chased him. Do you know how I felt when he fell for you? Humiliated. He never did tell you, did he? That I fancied him and made a complete ass of myself . . .'

'Oh . . . Vickie.' On the brink of sympathetic tears, Kerry sprang up, ready to comfort her. 'I had no idea, and I'm sure you didn't make a fool of yourself.'

'Don't be kind, Kerry. I couldn't stomach that at this moment,' Vickie snapped, her composed face contorting with strong emotion as she turned her back. 'I took that job in Venice because I wanted to cause trouble. I hated him because he didn't want me. I wasn't good enough. I'd been around. Hell, so had he been . . . but the old double-standard was made by men like Alex.' The words were pouring from her now in staccato bursts. 'He wouldn't have married you if he hadn't been the first.'

Kerry sank down again, thunderstruck by what Vickie had hidden from her. She recalled Vickie's pettish refusal to be her bridesmaid, Alex's unrelenting coolness towards the sister she admired. The facts had been there before her, the suggestion of something that did not ring quite true, but she had been so full of loving Alex, she had been blind. She bled for the pain she had unwittingly caused Vickie. It was one thing not to attract a man, another for the same man to marry a kid sister. And Vickie had never had any trouble in getting the men she wanted. She was a very beautiful woman. Alex's indifference must have hit her hard.

'I wish you'd told me about this a long time ago,' she said unhappily. 'I used to talk all the time about Alex. It must have upset you.'

Vickie stubbed out her cigarette, and immediately lit another with an unsteady hand. 'What upset me was the way he felt about you. He was besotted and it sickened me. But he had one Achilles heel. He was scared stiff your feelings were going to change and you were going to grow out of him,' she continued jerkily. 'That's why he was so jealous and possessive. He had worked out for himself that if you never got any rope without him or one of his sisters, you couldn't get up to much. The night of my birthday when you phoned him, I was listening on the extension . . . and I heard every dirty label he attached to me. Of course, can you blame him? Even after the wedding, I made it clear that I was available!'

Twin spots of livid colour burnt over Vickie's cheekbones. Kerry looked sickly away from her. Her sister spared herself no pride in the confession. She remembered Alex's blazing anger that night on the phone. He had succinctly summed up his opinion of Vickie's frequent and casual affairs. It must have been very painful for Vickie to listen to the character assassination.

'To give him his due, he had just cause. Alex is quick,' Vickie conceded. 'He knew how I felt about him, and he despised me for it. I was furious that night and very bitter. I had had a lot to drink, although I'm not using that as an excuse . . . Jeff had stupidly put something in your drink to try and brighten you up a bit. When I found out I was angry with him, but by then you had already collapsed. I hauled you up to bed before twelve and you were out for the count . . . '

'But you said I was up to all hours drinking . . . ' Kerry whispered.

'It still hasn't sunk in yet, has it? I lied! I told you a pack of lies!' she extended rawly. 'I never went to bed. I stayed up all night with the last of my guests. When I saw Alex's car drawing up down below, I decided to get my own back. I wasn't thinking of you or the future or anything. It was an impulse. It was Alex I wanted to hurt. Jeff was still drunk. I told him it was a practical joke. He tore into your room, threw off his clothes and got into that bed beside you. He was there all of two minutes before Alex arrived.'

'No . . . it couldn't have been like that . . . ' Kerry's tongue seemed too large for her mouth, the syllables of her dazed interruption dragging.

Vickie drew deep on her cigarette and stared at her. 'It was. Jeff never laid a finger on you, not a single finger. I ran to the front door, threw it wide, looked suitably shocked and Alex leapt at the bait. I got the biggest thrill of my life watching Alex's face when he saw you and Jeff in that bed. It was pure farce, but it knocked Alex flat.' She relived it without pleasure. Indeed, her voice was wooden. 'I didn't know he was going to go right off his head like he did. I thought he'd put it together for himself. He was always so damned clever about everything else. He should have smelt a rat the minute he got over the shock. But he didn't.'

In the grip of astonishment, Kerry was speechless. The sordid episode which had wrecked her marriage and nearly destroyed her had been a cruel, spur-of-the-moment practical joke! Nothing had happened. All these years she had carried round this soiled feeling of shame. And nothing had happened!

'How could I have known that he would walk out on you and wall himself up?' Vickie demanded stridently. 'I didn't know what to do. I was scared. I would have ended up the family outcast. He would have ruined my career, too. All over his over-reaction to a crazy, childish joke! As if I'd have let him in if you'd really been in bed with somebody!'

'So you kept quiet.' Kerry could not conceal her revulsion. 'You let me go through hell. In fact, you *watched* me go through it. I hated myself and I didn't even do anything!' Her voice rose steeply.

Vickie collapsed down opposite, her eyes anguished. 'It all just mushroomed, it got too big for me to handle. But I had to tell you now, I had to get it off my chest. I couldn't see you going back to him because you thought you owed him the sacrifice . . .'

'Or did you tell me because you couldn't stand the idea of me being Kerry Veranchetti again?' she countered in helpless suspicion.

Vickie flinched visibly. 'OK, I deserve that and more, but I got over my jealousy and my infatuation a very long time ago. Don't you understand what I went through, too? I was terrified of telling anybody.' Tears streaked her sister's face. 'Once it was done I didn't know how to stop the shockwaves spreading.'

But she had still protected herself. Kerry lifted her head proudly. 'You have to go to Alex and tell him the truth. Do you hear me? And while we're on the subject, what about the mysterious Jeff, who so conveniently disappeared?' she stabbed grimly.

'Jeff?' Vickie's eyes slewed back to her in shock. 'What's he got to do with it?'

Either her sister was very naïve, or this was sarcasm.

Now she had the whole story, Kerry found Vickie's insistence that Jeff had been a stranger somewhat harder to swallow. 'Did you really ask a complete stranger to take part in your joke?' she demanded uncertainly. 'When I think about it, I find it hard to credit that you've neither heard of him nor seen him since. You know hundreds of people in the fashion industry, you're both in the same trade. Are you telling me that you couldn't track him down if you tried?'

'Track him down?' Vickie ejaculated. 'What for?'

'Obviously in the hope that I could persuade him to back up your story for Alex. Jeff hasn't got any reason to lie, has he? Have you really never seen him since?' Kerry pressed less hopefully.

'Never . . . my God, it's a big world out there! He mightn't even be a photographer now, and even if I could . . . help, why should he risk life and limb to help you? Can you imagine the kind of revenge Alex would take?'

Kerry's brows pleated. 'You're filled with amazing concern for somebody you don't know, aren't you? *What is his name?*' she prompted tautly.

'I don't know! I don't know a thing about him!' Vickie practically shouted at her, and it was obvious that for her this situation had got out of control. Kerry was talking about possibilities she had never foreseen, and suggesting taking the entire affair beyond these four walls, an affair moreover which showed Vickie to poor advantage.

'I don't believe you,' Kerry admitted wearily.

'Alex wouldn't even believe me. Why try to drag anybody else into it? Even if I could find him for you, what good would it do? I'm damned if I would face Alex. He didn't trust you, that was his problem,' Vickie argued vehemently. 'Not mine. And the way he treated you afterwards showed you what Alex was really like. He's a bastard.'

'You won't tell Alex, will you?' Kerry read the answer in her evasive gaze and experienced a spasm of sick disgust. 'Well, may God forgive you, Vickie, because I never will. How could you have been such a cold, selfish schemer? What did I ever do to you?' she whispered.

Vickie just sat there, pale and trembling but silent.

Kerry got up, defeated but angry. 'Let me tell you something else; you were in love with Alex. If you couldn't have him, you didn't want me to have him either. That's what it all came down to four years ago.'

She walked out of the apartment, grimly and impotently convinced that Vickie was withholding information about Jeff. Four years ago, it had suited Vickie very nicely to have no Jeff available to refute her lies. Kerry's head was reeling dizzily. Vickie. To even credit that Vickie had saved her own skin and pride at the expense of her marriage devastated her. It was as if her sister had suddenly become a stranger to her. Kerry could not forget, forgive or even begin to understand how her sister could have remained silent when she realised Alex intended to divorce her.

Her sister just hadn't been able to hold on to the dark secret any longer. Her nerves had given way. Kerry remembered her nervous brittle manner at the hospital. Vickie had been scared that, if Alex and Kerry finally got together, her duplicity might somehow be revealed. How could it have been? Kerry had never understood why she should recall not a single thing between feeling drowsy and waking up. But she had never suspected that her drink had been doctored. Vickie had told her that she had over-indulged. Kerry had had no cause to disbelieve her, and Vickie had staged a very good act of sympathy that morning. Perhaps she had enjoyed seeing Kerry at the mercy of shock and horror. Kerry wondered painfully if she would ever be able to believe in anybody again.

When she stepped out of the car at the vicarage, Nicky came running to her. 'Can we go home now?' he demanded.

'Yes.' Again she manoeuvred out of any long chats with her parents. They accepted that she had a great deal to do, and Vickie's revelations had made Kerry eager to be away from their unworldly contentment.

As Nicky chattered on the drive back to the cottage, a strange new lightness of heart began to lift her out of her introspection. The nightmare in her conscience had suddenly been banished. The shadows were gone. The guilt was gone. In a peculiar way, Vickie had set her free.

'Granny said that you and me and Daddy are all going to live together,' Nicky relayed excitedly.

She tautened, sucked back willy-nilly to the present. How could she turn in her tracks now? She had no proof. Would Alex even believe Vickie, or would he think that Kerry was rather pitifully trying to cover up too late? A surge of savage hostility encased her then. The tables had been turned. She could hate Alex now without feeling guilty about it. He had judged her without a hearing. Suddenly she was in so much conflict that she couldn't think straight. She was sick and tired of being a victim. Vickie had made her one, Alex had followed suit with a cruelty foreign to Kerry's softer nature.

If she married Alex she would still be paying for a crime she had not commited. She had already paid a hundred times over. Dammit, why should she be victimised again?

Her fingers hovered over the phone to contact the driver and tell him to return her to the vicarage. She saw herself walking in and laying the whole story before them. Simultaneously, she saw herself destroying her family. It would still come down to her word against Vickie's. It would tear their parents apart to see their two daughters engaged in such bitter conflict. She couldn't do that to them. She couldn't risk her father's health, either. Her hand fell heavily back on to her lap. Alex had won, after all. Alex always won.

The wedding took place five days later. Vickie took sick last moment, and phoned the vicarage to say she was down with gastric 'flu. Steven had spent most of the intervening period begging Kerry to tell him what was wrong with her. On several occasions she nearly broke down and spilt it all out: her ever-mounting sense of injustice. Four years, she kept on thinking, four wretched, miserable years that had practically crippled her emotionally because she had been enslaved by her own guilt.

She was like a statue during the brief ceremony in a London register office. They came out to a barrage of photographers. The Veranchetti rematch, someone quipped. Alex was all smiles, the two-faced swine that he was. Antipathy raced through her in a stormy wave, and as he met her eyes, his narrowed perceptively.

'What's wrong?' he enquired.

Kerry almost laughed. What's wrong? she thought wildly. Oh, there's nothing wrong, Alex. You forced me into this marriage, you're forcing me to share my son, you're forcing me back into a life-style I hated . . . really, Alex why should there be anything wrong?

'Are you feeling all right?' She guessed he could afford the solicitous look. He thought he had won. Well, he hadn't won. All hell would break loose if he dared to try and exert his marital rights.

He carried her firmly off into the car, away from the loud voices asking quite incredibly impertinent questions. 'I have a headache,' she lied.

'Stress.'

What the heck would he know about stress? She turned her flushed profile aside. There was still the meal with her parents to be got through with a civilised show.

'Why didn't Glenn attend the wedding, if he was such a good friend?' Alex drawled softly.

'I try not to involve my friends in burlesque shows.'

'I'm sorry that you feel that way about our wedding.'

'What wedding?' Her green eyes flashed at him. Although she had promised herself that she would not start until her parents were safely off-scene, she could no longer control her ire. 'You got me here at the point of a gun. Why the polite hypocrisy? I don't need it.'

His lustrous dark eyes rested on her unreadably. 'I don't want to argue with you today.'

Why was there something special about today? Her contempt showed, and his aggressive jawline set. For the space of a heartbeat she thought Alex was about to lose his cool. But his thick, dark lashes screened his gaze. She admired his control. The limousine filtered to a halt in front of the hotel. She pinned a smile to her lips for her parents' benefit. Another couple of of hours and the need even to smile would be over.

CHAPTER SIX

THEY were flying straight to Rome. It seemed that Alex could not wait to parade his bride to the family again.

'It will be easier if it is done immediately,' he pronounced during the flight. He actually reached for Kerry's clenched fingers. 'Believe me, no one will say anything to hurt your feelings.'

His family could not afford to offend him; Alex either employed them or supported them. They would have had to accept Frankensteins's Bride with a smile had Alex made the demand! Her generous mouth thinned. Well, she wasn't the trusting and naïve teenager she had been on her last visit. Nobody would intimidate her this time.

'Is it the prospect of meeting my family again which is worrying you?'

She raised a brow. 'Nothing's worrying me.'

Nicky climbed up on her knee and planted himself bodily between them. 'This is my mummy.' There was a miniature Veranchetti stress to the possessive tone employed. Ever since Nicky had adjusted to the sight of his parents together, he had been growing increasingly less certain about whether or not he liked the combination.

'And my wife,' Alex murmured.

'She's not.' Nicky's mouth came out in a pout. 'I'm going to marry her when I get growed up. You've got Helena.'

FIRST-CLASS ROMANCE

Mail This Heart TODAY!

And We'll Deliver:

**4 FREE BOOKS
A FREE BRACELET WATCH
PLUS
A SURPRISE MYSTERY BONUS
TO YOUR DOOR!**

HARLEQUIN DELIVERS
FIRST-CLASS ROMANCE—
DIRECT TO YOUR DOOR

Mail the Heart sticker on the postpaid order card today and you'll receive:

—**4 new Harlequin Presents®novels—FREE**
—**a lovely bracelet watch—FREE**
—**and a surprise mystery bonus—FREE**

But that's not all. You'll also get:

Money-Saving Home Delivery
When you subscribe to Harlequin Reader Service, the excitement, romance and faraway adventures of these novels can be yours for previewing in the convenience of your own home at less than cover prices. Every month we'll deliver 8 new books right to your door. If you decide to keep them, they'll be yours for only $1.99* each. That's 26¢ less than the cover price. And there is *no* extra charge for shipping and handling! There is no obligation to buy—you can cancel Reader Service privileges at any time by writing "cancel" on your statement or by returning a shipment of books to us at our expense.

Free Monthly Newsletter
It's the indispensable insider's look at our most popular writers and their upcoming novels. Now you can have a behind-the-scenes look at the fascinating world of Harlequin! It's an added bonus you'll look forward to every month!

Special Extras—FREE
Because our home subscribers are our most valued readers, we'll also be sending you additional free gifts from time to time in our monthly book shipments, as a token of our appreciation.

OPEN YOUR MAILBOX TO A WORLD OF LOVE AND ROMANCE EACH MONTH. JUST COMPLETE, DETACH AND MAIL YOUR FREE OFFER CARD TODAY!

*Terms and prices subject to change without notice.

FREE OFFER CARD

4 FREE BOOKS

**FREE BRACELET
WATCH**

**FREE MYSTERY
BONUS**

PLACE
HEART
STICKER
HERE

**MONEY-SAVING
HOME DELIVERY**

**FREE FACT-FILLED
NEWSLETTER**

**MORE SURPRISES
THROUGHOUT THE
YEAR—FREE**

☑ **YES!** Please send me four Harlequin Presents®
novels, *free*, along with my free bracelet watch
and my free mystery gift, as explained on the opposite
page.   108 CIH CAN3

NAME _____

ADDRESS _____ APT. _____

CITY _____ STATE _____

ZIP CODE _____

Offer limited to one per household and
not valid to current Harlequin Presents
subscribers. All orders subject to approval.

MAIL THE POSTPAID CARD TODAY!

PRINTED IN U.S.A.

Remember! To receive your free books, bracelet watch and mystery gift, return the postpaid card below. But don't delay!

DETACH AND MAIL CARD TODAY.

If offer card has been removed, write to: Harlequin Reader Service, 901 Fuhrmann Blvd., P.O. Box 1867, Buffalo, NY 14269-1867

MAIL THE POSTPAID CARD TODAY!

BUSINESS REPLY CARD

First Class   Permit No. 717   Buffalo, NY

Postage will be paid by addressee

Harlequin Reader Service®
901 Fuhrmann Blvd.
P.O. Box 1867
Buffalo, NY 14240-9952

NO POSTAGE
NECESSARY
IF MAILED
IN THE
UNITED STATES

Kerry forced a laugh. Alex surveyed her over the top of Nicky's dark, curly head in cool question. 'I don't find that funny.'

'It makes pretty clear sense to him. He's seen you with too many different women,' Kerry riposted drily.

'Helena happens to be an eleven-year-old,' he interposed. 'And the women you talk about are at an end now.'

She shrugged as Nicky slid down restlessly and crossed the cabin to play with the jigsaw she had set out for him. 'I wouldn't speak too soon,' she replied. 'After all, I'm not going to share a bedroom with you again. Touch me and I'll disappear into thin air, Alex. I swear it. You can't have me watched all the time.'

Long fingers tipped up her chin. 'Don't utter foolish threats.'

'It's not a foolish threat. It's what will happen,' she informed him steadily, her eyes icy-cold. 'You've got your son, you've got a wife who will behave like a wife in public, but in private, as far as I am concerned, the act dies.'

'You realise that you are about to turn our marriage into a battle?' he raked in undertone back to her, his mouth taut. '*Dio*, when I was prepared to try and put everything in the past where it belongs, you begin to cause trouble. It won't work, *cara*, I warn you.'

She swallowed with difficulty. 'Content yourself with what you've got, Alex. It's all you're going to get.'

Unhidden anger gleamed in his narrowed scrutiny. 'Don't start it up again.'

'You started it. You got us both into this marriage,' she reminded him.

He sprang upright and strode up to the built-in bar,

where he barked at the steward, who hurried to serve him. He looked ready to commit murder. Golden brown eyes arrowed piercingly over her coolly composed face, and against her will she trembled. She had had to tell him before tonight. Perhaps she had not employed particular tact. But there really wasn't a diplomatic way of telling Alex that he was barred from his wife's bedroom. He behaved as if he owned her body and soul. He always had. And he only wanted to exert his rights over her sexually in revenge. He had told her that with unforgettable candour. She was amazed that he could still behave as if she was the one being unreasonable.

'Daddy's cross,' Nicky whispered when she got down to help him with his puzzle. 'Did I do somefin' wrong?'

'No.' She gave him a guilty little hug. Alex was emanating enough hostility to carry them to Rome without jet engines.

'Did *you* do somefin' wrong?' Nicky asked guilelessly.

Reluctantly, she approached Alex. 'Nicky is picking up the atmosphere,' she reproved tautly.

His fingers came down on her tense shoulder and she froze. His other hand splayed across her narrow back as he drew her firmly up against him. Deliberately taking advantage of her inability to struggle, he tasted her angrily parted lips. She stopped breathing, she was so busy fighting the danger of response. He laughed with throaty enjoyment against her lips, and merely deepened the pressure.

'Stop it!' Nicky screeched hurling himself at Alex's legs. 'That's my mummy, leave her alone!'

Alex released her and dropped down lithely in front of their son. She had expected him to lose his temper, but he soothed Nicky and lifted him up, leaving her out of what appeared to be a man-to-man exchange. Annoyance snaked through her. It was the first time she had ever seen her child turn in his distress to someone else.

Nicky returned with enormous, hurt, dark eyes to stare at her.

'What on earth did you say to him?' she demanded of Alex.

'That I won't be leaving you alone. What did you expect me to say?' Alex enquired with a brilliant smile. 'What he just saw he has to get used to. He's likely to see a lot of it in the future. That's a fact of life.'

'Not of mine,' she assured him through gritted teeth.

It was pouring with rain when they landed in Rome. The Veranchetti home there was an enormous, impressive town house behind high walls. Kerry was quiet as the car wafted them through the gates. The courtyard was full of opulent vehicles. The family had evidently turned out *en masse*. Her own tension mounted another notch.

'It will be all right,' Alex said gently. 'I promise you that.'

'I'm not worried. They're mostly a set of hidebound troglodytes with too much money,' she parried wildly.

'What's a troglodyte?' In the echoing hall with its alcoves and tall Chinese vases, Alex bent his dark head teasingly.

She reddened. 'It's not very complimentary.'

A brown forefinger confidently brushed a straying strand of vibrant hair back from her cheekbone, and his breath fanned her cheek. 'It's like a sunset,

your hair. A glorious, multicoloured sunset,' he
growled half under his breath. 'The very first time I
saw you I imagined it cascading over white
pillows . . .'

The tip of her tongue snaked out to moisten her dry
lips. They had gone from troglodytes to sunsets to
pillows. He lowered his head and ran the tip of his
own tongue erotically along the same path, hunger
burnishing his golden eyes, a devouring,
smoulderingly sexual hunger which tightened his
hard bone structure and sent Kerry into shaken
retreat. 'Later . . . ' Alex practically tasted the word.

No, there wasn't going to be a later. Her colour
high, she spun and recognised the tall, dark young
man standing watching them. 'Mario?'

'Kerry.'

Alex's youngest brother bent to kiss her cheek.
While she had been away, he had grown to manhood
from a lanky and boyish sixteen. He backed off again
awkwardly, stuck for the verbal social niceties to fit
the occasion. Nicky streaked past them. *'Nonna!'* he
hollered at the top of his voice.

On the threshold of the crowded drawing-room
Kerry stilled in surprise. Her son went hurtling
cheerfully towards the thin woman with the patrician
features seated in a wing-backed chair by the fire. His
grandmother, Athene. He gave her an exuberant hug
and grabbed her hand. 'Come and meet my mummy.'

Oh, my God, Kerry thought, feeling Alex's hand
welding to her spine like a bar preventing retreat.
'He's her favourite,' he divulged.

But only next to her firstborn son, Alex. Athene
looked upon Alex with a fierce pride which only
dimmed when her eyes slid to the wife by his side. A
cool kiss was pressed to her cheek. 'You are welcome,'

Athene said graciously.

She was threaded through the gathered cliques. Alex was one of six children, with three sisters and two brothers. Between them they had about thirty offspring, or so it had always seemed to Kerry. Both the sisters and the daughter-in-law conformed in the Veranchetti clan. They maintained their husbands' homes and raised children and shopped as if there was no tomorrow . . . real exciting stuff, Kerry thought wryly. Entering this old-style family was like stepping back a century in women's rights to a time where the men were still men and the women were delighted they were. Alex's rule here was supreme. By some quixotic quirk of heredity, none of his siblings had an ounce of his drive and self-assurance. They followed him like a flock of sheep. His sisters adored him and his brothers admired him. His opinion was sought on the most minor decisions.

The general warmth of her reception surprised her. Athene's frosty smiles were the equivalent of a red carpet. It seemed that her supposed infidelity remained a secret within the family circle. Her discomfiture eased and Nicky bounced along beside her, showing off by introducing her to all and sundry.

'Nicky is so like you,' Alex's middle sister, Carina, exclaimed.

'Me?' Kerry laughed. She only ever saw Alex when she looked at her son. His amber-brown eyes, black hair and lean, above average height all echoed his paternity.

'Your smile . . . he has your smile and your liveliness.' Carina patted the seat beside her. 'How does it feel to be back?'

But I'm not back, I'm only passing through . . . where? Dear heaven, where were they spending the night?

'A little strange,' Kerry admitted truthfully. Yet there was a subtle difference to her own responses. She was no longer overwhelmed by the opulence and the formality which Athene insisted upon. It wasn't Kerry and it never would be, but she didn't feel a failure simply because she did not fit the family female mould. It was over four years. A woman did a lot of maturing in that time, she acknowledged.

'I am pleased that Alex and you are together again,' Carina declared carefully. 'Mamma was . . . er . . . disturbed by the divorce, and Alex cut himself off from the family for a long time. He . . . how you say . . . ? Dug himself into work. Alex, he's like Mamma. Too strong . . . you understand?'

'No,' she said frankly.

Carina moved a plump beringed hand. 'He can't bend, he can't talk of what he really feels . . . you know? But where would we be without Alex to tell us what to do?'

Heaven? 'I don't know,' said Kerry dutifully.

'Alex is the clever one in the family. We were lost when he was too busy for us, but I think we learned that Alex had a life to lead of his own,' Carina confided, her round, dark eyes resting ruefully on Kerry's face. 'Before, if he was not at the office or abroad, you would find him having to help one of us . . . eh?'

Kerry nodded honestly. Alex had always been very much in demand. If they bought a new house, if someone was ill, if there was marital dissension or problems in business—they called Alex. In the past she had resented those constant encroachments into what little time they had together as a couple.

'I think you will find this has changed,' Carina murmured, and her sincerity made Kerry feel uncomfortable, for the less she saw of Alex in their present relationship, the happier she would be.

After dinner, served in the lofty-ceilinged dining-room, Kerry inwardly accepted that they were obviously expected to stay the night here. Coffee was served in the drawing-room, and she found herself seated with Athene, everybody else steering a rather deliberate passage to leave them in privacy.

'We have had our differences in the past,' Athene delivered with a regal inclination of her silvered head. 'But you are Alex's wife again now and these must be set aside. I want you to know that I did not want the divorce. I begged Alex to reconsider. Our family has never had a divorce before, and you were expecting my grandson. In the light of your remarriage, it is clear that Alex should have listened to me.' Before she could reply, Athene added smoothly, 'We will not speak of this again.'

The conversation became general, and Alex's other two sisters, Maria and Contadina joined them. As usual, all the men were on the other side of the room. Kerry's mind began to wander restively. She would have to share a bedroom with Alex tonight. Some wedding night it was going to be, she reflected tensely.

'You're in your usual rooms,' Athene informed her later on, and Kerry's cheeks warmed.

She mounted the stairs, smothering a yawn. The resident nanny had marshalled Carina's children and Nicky off to bed earlier. It was comforting to find their bedroom suite changed beyond recognition. She felt less like a woman in a timewarp. Then she had to admit that there was very little left of the happy, gauche and outspoken teenager she had been when she first came to this house. With hindsight, she disliked Athene less for the callous and cold snubs dealt to her behind Alex's back.

What a ghastly shock she must have been to Athene's snobbish and ambitious hopes for her eldest son! Alex's bride had been a chirpy teenager, who wore her thoughts and her feelings on her sleeve and hurled herself into Alex's arms when he came home, regardless of who was present. Her confidence had not lasted. She had lived on the periphery of Alex's busy schedule, and the shopping trips, the endless rounds of polite socialising which had filled his sisters' days, these had driven her up the walls with boredom.

'Alex . . . of all my sons,' she had once heard Athene proclaim to a close friend. 'Marrying a little nobody with no breeding and no background. She will always be an embarrassment to him. Wherever she goes she is late. Her taste in clothes is indescribable, and she gossips with the maids . . . '

In remembrance, a rueful grin lit Kerry's lips. How terribly lonely she had been here, and yet how afraid that the criticisms were just ones, But the memories no longer bit with venom. She had let her insecurities grow out of proportion, and Athene, still reeling in those early days from Alex's choice of bride, had received a vengeful pleasure from pointing out her failings. Once they had moved to Florence, Kerry had evaded every effort Alex made to draw his family back into their lives. It must have been very hard for him. Naturally he had thought she was being unreasonable. Athene had never dared to be malicious when he was around.

Why was she thinking this way? Why was she seeing her own faults and making excuses for his? He had neglected her. He had refused to see that she wasn't the rich idle wife type. When she had become pregnant the sense of being trapped had grown stronger, for Alex had used her condition as an excuse to keep her tied to the house in Florence those first few months. Vickie had had a strong influence on Kerry then. It had not been difficult for Vickie to heighten Kerry's resentment of Alex's possessiveness. But Alex had grown up with a mother and three sisters who automatically deferred to him. If he had loved her . . . how could he really have loved her? she asked herself cynically, irritated by the tenor of her thoughts.

He came into the room and shed his jacket. She kept on reading her magazine doggedly.

'This won't work,' he breathed. 'We can't live like strangers and hope to give our son a happy environment.'

'You should have thought of that.' His reasonable tone, the sombre cast of his appraisal were, however, disconcerting. She had expected a return of the anger and the obduracy he had briefly displayed during the flight.

'No.' Cool fingers twitched up the magazine and tossed it arrogantly aside. 'You should have thought of that before you shared my bed a few nights ago. We cannot for ever throw recriminations at each other. What is done is done. This marriage is a new beginning, not a continuation of hostilities. I will accept nothing less.' The hawk-gold gaze rested calmly on her infuriated face. 'That is all I have to say for now.'

He strolled into the bathroom, leaving her a prey to temper. Alex had turned sanctimonious. At least in his contempt and anger and need for revenge that night at the apartment, he had been honest with her. But now he realised that he had been too honest and that she had more backbone than he had given her credit for possessing. Naturally, he didn't want a wife who loathed him. He didn't want the arguments, either. He could afford to be generous now that he had got what he wanted. Having taken her in lust, honour was now more or less satisfied. If he could convince her that he was now magnanimously prepared for a fresh start without retrospective glances into the past, what did it really cost him?

Alex could be very charming and very credible. Until she had offended, she had had no idea that nine-tenths of the real Alex was hidden beneath an indulgent and sophisticated surface. Having learnt painfully at first hand how merciless and hard he could be, she must never be taken in by pleasantries again. He couldn't possibly be practising sincerity. Not after the cruel intimidation and derision he had employed to get her to the altar. She had to admit that from the moment that ring went on her finger again, Alex had been extraordinarily civil. But then that was for Nicky's sake and his family's. No, she couldn't afford to trust him. At heart, he despised her still.

When he came to bed, Kerry was pretending to be asleep.

'Goodnight,' he murmured softly, without coming near her.

In the darkness she grimaced. He certainly wasn't burning with desire for her! Anger and revenge had powered his previous hunger into a physical catharsis. Those fierce emotions slaked, only masculine pride would make Alex demand repetition. It would never happen again, she promised herself. Now that she was free of the shackles of the old guilt, she was her own person again, and self-preservation came first.

'Greece?' she mumbled sleepily.

He had shaken her awake, and with difficulty. She had finally dropped off about four in the morning. Opening her eyes to Alex's leaping vitality and the intimacy of the bedroom scene sharply off-balanced her. He had further dismayed her by announcing that they were leaving this morning for the island of Kordos, which had come to Alex by inheritance via his Greek grandfather. 'Greece?' she said again.

Alex shifted a broad shoulder sheathed in white silk. 'We have to spend some time together.'

'To satisfy convention?' she taunted.

His perfectly chiselled mouth firmed. 'We need time to bridge the gap of years. Time to relax and become acquainted with each other again, if you like, and we certainly do not require an audience while we accomplish that feat.'

'I don't want to go to Greece.'

'That's unfortunate,' he murmured drily. 'We are going, and when we leave the island, we will return to our home in Florence. I still have the house there. You're going to be late for breakfast if you don't get up,' he completed, sweeping up his jacket and departing.

Alex, you rotten, manipulative swine, she thought. He had saved it all up and delivered it as stated fact. A honeymoon in Greece and a return to Florence. It was a shock to learn that he still owned the house they had once chosen together. She had assumed that he would have sold Casa del Fiore.

She had to rush to get downstairs in time for breakfast, and Nicky was nowhere to be seen.

'Mario has taken Nicky and Carina's boys out for breakfast. He's also going to take them to the zoo,' Alex supplied. 'I explained to Nicky that we would be away for a while. He will have plenty to occupy him here.'

As it sunk in that Nicky was not coming to Kordos with them, disbelief fired her almond-shaped green eyes.

'Alex and you need some peace,' Athene ruled down the table. 'And Nicky is too attached to you.'

'How can a child be too attached to his mother?' Kerry enquired spiritidely. 'We will talk about this in private.' Alex threw her a warning glance.

'Mamma did not mean to offend,' Carina soothed under the general cover of conversation. 'But it is right that you should have time to spend as a couple before you become a family again.'

Kerry set her teeth together. How dared Alex arrange to leave Nicky behind without even consulting her? Indeed, having foreseen her objections, he had simply chosen to go over her head.

'I hate to tell you this, but Nicky is becoming a spoilt little brat,' Alex dropped when everybody else had deserted the table. 'When he was with you he had all your attention, and when he was with me it was the same. I could not play the strict father then because I was afraid to destroy the relationship I did have with him. Everybody has spoilt Nicky because we were divorced.'

'But that's going to change, right?' she gathered shakily.

'Gradually it will, as he adjusts to the presence of both of us.' He refused to rise to her anger, and he sighed. 'You know as well as I do that what I say is true, but the main reason I made the decision that he should remain here is that if it were otherwise, he would inevitably become aware of the conflict between us, and I will not have that happen.'

Unwillingly she recalled Nicky's boisterous behaviour the night before. It was true that he was much too used to being the centre of attention, but she still felt that she was being punished through her son for standing up to Alex yesterday. How could she feel otherwise? She had no wish to develop a closer relationship with Alex. It was an impossibility, and in its own way a potential trap. If she ever opened up to Alex again, he would hurt her, and she couldn't take that a second time. How did he even have the gall to imply that it was her duty to fulfil his expectations?

But she was forgetting that she was a second-class citizen in Alex's eyes. Remarrying an adulterous wife was no mean concession in his book. He undoubtedly thought that she ought to be eating grateful and humble pie for the rest of her days. Yes, sir, no, sir, three bags full, sir.

'Even had I discussed this with you, you would have said no,' he continued. 'Ask yourself how we can deal with Nicky when we are still at each other's throats? And then tell me I am being cruel to him.'

Colour fluctuated wildly in her cheeks. 'This is simply blackmail in another form,' she condemned.

His eyes narrowed, his jaw clenching. 'I would not use our son in that way,' he contradicted icily.

'You used him in that contract, didn't you? You keep on forgetting that I am here against my will,' she whispered dully.

Alex thrust back his chair and walked out of the room, rather than giving vent to his temper. Kerry went upstairs, feeling curiously empty of satisfaction. He hadn't liked the truth being hurled at him. And, much as it galled her to admit it, she had made a pointless reminder. She could talk about duress until the cows came home, but they would still be married.

'How long are we to stay on Kordos?' she asked during the flight to Athens.

'One week . . . two.' He eyed her with the cool implacability. 'When we return for Nicky we won't have this atmosphere between us.'

'I never realised that you believed in miracles.

The sardonic look she earned washed pink into her cheeks. 'You will make the effort that I am making. Neither of us could possibly be content in the mockery of a relationship that you appear to want,' he asserted.

Her soft mouth moved tremulously. Oh, Alex, you really had it all once and you threw it away, she thought sadly. She had loved him very deeply. She had had him on a tall pedestal, and she had never ceased to marvel that he had chosen her. But he had broken her heart and her spirit. He had taught her how to be bitter.

Her hostility had ironically been exacerbated by Vickie's confession. Was it fair of her to feel that he should have given her a hearing? In his position, would she have? She doubted whether she could have walked away when denying Alex meant denying everything that was important to her. Thank God that it wasn't like that for her still, she allowed gratefully.

Kerry had never visited Kordos before. A trip had been suggested on several occasions, but business or family had always intervened. She watched the jewelled green speck Alex pointed out suddenly expand in size against the deep blue of the Aegean. A small and picturesque fishing village straggled round the harbour. The helicopter cast a long shadow over the dark pine trees which shrouded the steep hills behind the village. Up on the cliffs sprawled a long, white villa with a red-tiled roof. It was ringed on its rocky height by flagstone terraces. They dropped down on the helipad set into the level ground to the front.

The staff had emerged from the villa to greet them. Sofia and Spiros, who ran the house, and a gaggle of dark-eyed, giggly maids were duly introduced to her. But it was Alex who guided her into the shade of the house ahead of them and said, 'I will show you to your room.'

'I'm actually getting one of my own?'

'Why should I wish to share a room with you?' A satiric brow quirked. 'I, too, like my privacy. I do not deny you yours.'

It was a concession she had not expected and nor had Sofia, the housekeeper, who protested that the room was not properly prepared. He left Kerry alone, as she struggled against an unjustifiable tide of pain and despondency. Why on earth should she feel insulted? It was a step in the right direction, removing them from the dangerous intimacy she had feared. She stared out of the arched windows at the magnificent view of rock and sea and skyline merging majestically together.

Alex reappeared a few minutes later and insisted upon showing her around before she changed for dinner. She duly admired the clean, tiled floors scattered with priceless Persian rugs, and the air of comfort and tradition which adhered to the sparse furnishings in their plain, earthy colours. After that she took herself off for a short nap and ended up rushing to get dressed in time for dinner.

'You look rested,' Alex saluted her mockingly with his glass. 'Has it improved your humour?'

In exasperation, she stiffened. 'There was nothing wrong with my mood. How am I supposed to react to a place like this? What are we going to do here?'

Alex burst out laughing, white teeth flashing against brown skin. 'Do you really want me to tell you?'

It was a setting for lovers, not for two people who could hardly speak to each other civilly. 'All *I* plan to do here is read some of the books I brought with me,' she warned in dulcet dismissal.

He absorbed her mutinous face with arrogant amusement. 'You want to punish me for persuading you into my arms before the wedding. But it was inevitable that the force of our emotions would bring us together. It brought me peace . . .' he stressed. 'The past is over, *cara*. Why can't you accept that?'

Angrily, she began to eat. It had brought him peace. It had torn her apart. He had received the ego-boosting response he required from his recalcitrant wife. He had conquered his own distaste and her reluctance. He made no apology for the cruelty of his words to her that night. Why should he apologise? In his mind, he would always have the perfect excuse to employ that rapier tongue if she got out of hand. The past is over. No, he was wrong. The past had made the present for them both.

'I'm not sleeping with you, Alex,' she asserted.

'Inevitably you will. You see, you want me.' Golden eyes held hers steadily. 'Why should you be ashamed of that?'

How could he ask her that after his admission that he despised her?

'How many times must I tell you that the past is

finished?' His lean, strong features were harshly set. 'You made one mistake, but we both paid dearly for it. Some day I will forget that other day, but I promise that I will never throw it at you in anger again.'

Her mouth twisted. 'And what are you doing right now?' she flared.

He slammed his wine glass down. 'What do you think I am trying to do? I am trying to talk to you, I am trying to be civilised!' he gritted in the most uncivilised snarl.

'You're in the wrong century. I've had enough to eat.' She rose with unhurried grace and left the table.

In her room she paced the floor. She had almost screamed her innocence at him. But she would only have demeaned herself in his eyes. He would never believe her and she had no evidence. Naturally he saw no good reason why she shouldn't abandon herself to pure physical gratification in his bed. In the depths of Alex's subconscious would always lurk the reflection that if she could do so with a stranger, she certainly wasn't in a position to deny a husband.

When she emerged from her bathroom later, swathed in a light cream satin peignoir, Alex was reclining fully dressed on top of her neatly turned-down bed.

'What do you want?' she demanded.

He studied her tousled and damp appearance, the fiery hair tumbling round her heart-shaped face, the tight clasp of her fingers on the lace edges of the scanty covering. He took his time looking her over, a burnished glitter of desire brightening his dark eyes. A brilliant smile curved his mouth, making her vibrantly aware of the leashed sensuality coiled within his relaxed length. 'What do I want?' he echoed softly. 'Only to kiss you goodnight for the servants' benefit. You will come to me the next time we make love.'

'There won't be a next time,' she swore as he slid upright and folded his arms around her rigid body.

His lips feathered across hers, and she trembled long before the hard heat of his mouth properly engulfed the sweetness of her own. It was a taste of heaven and a taste of hellfire damnation all in one go. His hard thighs were imprinted against her softer curves as she leant inexorably closer to him, until he was holding her upright. She shivered violently in the unyielding possession of sensations infinitely stronger than she was, sensations that whispered and yet burned over every part of her. With a husky laugh, Alex gathered her up and deposited her down on the bed before freeing her.

He stepped back, his smile mocking the confusion she could not hide from him as she swam back to reality again. 'I do not think that you are cut out for the life of a celibate, *cara. Buona notte,*' he drawled with silken emphasis.

She groaned as the door shut. What was it about him, dammit, what was it about him that made him irresistible? Her hands curled into claws in the pillows. Her body had a blind spot where Alex was concerned. It was all this slothful eating and lying around and being waited on. Healthy activity was what she needed, and not of the kind Alex would suggest. There was no barrier there. It made no sense. She ought to freeze when he came close. But she didn't. The same powerful chemical attraction which had drawn her to him at eighteen was still there. Indeed, by some cruel twist of fate it had grown even stronger. She ought to be mature enough to handle

Alex's sensual magnetism and see it for what it was: a hangover from her misspent youth, a symptom of frustration. Unfortunately, none of her frantic efforts to explain away her response to him made it any easier to get to sleep.

CHAPTER SEVEN

KERRY slid out of bed, irritably pushing her hair off
her damp brow. A tide of dizziness went over her and
she groaned. It was the heat. Alex would die laughing
if he saw her like this. Hot, harassed, sleepless. She
curled up in the basketwork chair by the tall window.
It was their fifth day on the island. From dawn to
dusk, Alex had been charm personified. He had
broken the ice, in spite of her determination to remain
aloof. Somehow . . . heaven knew how, her sharp,
defensive retorts had begun to seem petty. They were
talking now without fighting. Of course not about
anything in particular. Safe things. Nicky, the house
in Florence, his business interests.

Her fingers rubbed at her tense neck muscles. She
had changed. She had changed from the moment
Vickie told her the truth. An inner strength had been
reborn, a surge of returning self-respect. It shook her
to admit that for four years she hadn't really cared
about anything but Nicky. She had just gone through
the motions, even in business, content to believe
herself independent of Alex, but too apathetic to
employ the effort of will required to lick Steven into
shape. She could have made a go of Antique Fayre.
Instead, she had let it limp along, and now there
would never be another chance to prove her own
mettle.

Last night they had attended a wedding in the
village as honoured guests, and amid the jubilant

mayhem of the celebration Alex had caught her to
him, amber eyes rampant with impatience. 'When . . .
hmm?' he had muttered. 'Why pretend? Deep down
inside you must know what you want. Or perhaps you
want to be told.'

The chauvinist emerged around nightfall. Alex
wasn't accustomed to waiting for anything he desired.
His restraint over the last few days had been sheathed
in a sardonic indulgence. The sexual charge in the
atmosphere was like an electric current. After all he
had done to her, how could she still want him?

The sight of Alex in a pair of low-slung, tight-fitting
shorts and nothing else was lethal enough to stop her
in her tracks. And he knew it. The torment was like a
knot jerking a little tighter every day. She couldn't
sleep because she ached for him. It infuriated her, it
outraged her pride, but she couldn't deny it. Alex
brought her alive as no other man ever had. An
unholy and primitive pleasure sent her pulses leaping
when he came close.

The clear, moonlit night beyond the glass was
dancing dark reflections on the shimmering surface of
the pool. It was three in the morning. Everybody
would be asleep. The water glimmered a silent
invitation. Leaving her room, she let herself out on to
the terrace. It was the impulse of a moment to shed
her nightdress and slide soundlessly down into the
gloriously cool depths. With a sigh of relief she floated
on to her back.

Alex would find himself a mistress. She could hug
her inviolability to the grave. She turned over and
began to swim. She didn't want him to have other
women. She had her pride, too. It was the woman
who looked the fool when her husband was
entertaining himself elsewhere. She ground her teeth

together at that humiliating reality. Lost within her own thoughts, she did not notice the ripples spreading on the water, signifying that she had company.

A pair of hands enclosed her waist. She gave a stifled gasp before Alex spun her round and pressed her back against the side of the pool, his hard, punishing mouth stealing her cry of bewilderment and fury. His lips roamed torturingly over her temples, her wet cheeks and down again to tantalise the corners of her mouth in a passionate barrage of burning caresses. Emerging from shock, Kerry planted her hands on his bare, muscular shoulders. 'Where did you come from?'

'I saw you from my bedroom window.' Alex dragged her small hands down and forced them to her sides. In the shadowy light, a hard-boned savagery clung to his taut, golden features. 'You flaunt yourself . . . you go too far . . . '

'F . . . Flaunt myself?' she echoed incredulously, mortified to learn that she had had an audience. 'You rotten . . . voyeur!'

His hands dug into the sodden mane of her hair. '*Dio*, I do not receive satisfaction from watching,' he scorned. 'But I'm entitled to take it when my wife plays at provocation.' His mouth connected hotly with a hollow in her throat. 'Your skin gleams like wet silver in this light.' His hands skimmed down, not quite steadily, to the full globes of her breasts. 'And I find that I am very much a man . . . '

'I never doubted it, but you promised!' she objected shrilly, a spasm of terrifying excitement shooting through her tremulous body.

'So I am human,' Alex grated in unashamed excuse, involved in a scorching trailpath across her smooth ivory shoulders, pausing to nip at her earlobe before stabbing his tongue in a hungry thrust between her lips, ands she quivered. Great breakers of anticipation washed over her in response.

The water eddied noisily round them as he pressed her closer still to his virile length. He did not have a stitch on either. A constricting pain tightened her stomach muscles on a wild, remorseless rush of pleasure.

'No . . . ' She fought her own weakness in desperation. Her palms braced against his shoulders in a fleeting gesture of protest, and then breathlessly, mindlessly, her hands began moving down in slow connection with his damp skin, her fingertips tangling in the black whorls of hair sprinkling the breadth of his chest. With an earthy groan of approval he pressed her hand down over his flat stomach to demonstrate his need, and she capitulated without thought. She was starved of him, almost frantic in the cruel hold of the desire he had unleashed within both of them.

Suddenly he was sweeping her up and wading towards the steps. He cast her down across the bed in his own unlit room, lowering himself down to her again with primal grace. 'When I saw you in that hospital, I knew it wasn't over. I looked at you,' he cited in a husky, accented growl. 'And I knew I had to have you again. You're in my blood like a fever and I'm in yours.'

His fingers spread her wet hair over the white woven counterpane, and he ran his hot, burnished gaze over her ivory slenderness, She felt like a sacrifice of old. It was insanity but she was spellbound. There was a wild, womanly joy to the discovery that Alex was as entrapped as she was. It seemed to make them equal. And when he bent over her, her lips parted by instinct to welcome his.

*　　*　　*

Kerry had a thumping headache when she woke up. She crawled weakly over the bed to squint in dull-eyed disbelief at the clock. She was back in her own room. Her nightdress lay on the chair as if she had never put it on, never taken it off. The curtains were firmly closed on the brilliant light of midday. It was as if the whole of the previous night had been a figment of her imagination. But the ache and the languor of her body told her otherwise.

Had it been a dream that there had been something magical about those hours? Why had she pretended to herself that she could resist Alex? He had put the heat on and she had scorched. She had burnt up in an inferno, incapable of denying him.

Ahead of her stretched a never-ending roundabout of falls from grace and morning-after attacks of conscience. She swallowed hard as she thought about all the affairs Alex had had since their divorce. Distaste rippled through her. She was her own worst enemy still. Why had she ever blamed him?

'Sleep well?' Alex lifted his blue-black head from a perusal of a Greek newspaper and watched her walk across the terrace.

'Yes.' Her eyes searched his cool, dark features in search of a smile, a greater warmth.

'Good.' Alex went back to his newspaper quickly. 'Could you tell Sofia that I'd appreciate lunch soon?'

Disconcertingly, her eyes glazed over with tears. She glanced down at the pale blue sundress she had carefully selected from her wardrobe and, spinning, she went back into the house. Last night Alex had slept with his wife. What had she expected? A magnificent bouquet of flowers on her pillow? Some romantic, loving gesture? What had happened might have been important to her, but it wasn't to him. She ought to have reminded herself that Alex's raw energy found a natural vent in sex. And, as he had said, why should he not use her as he had accused her of once using him?

She mumbled to Sofia about lunch and mentioned a headache in the same breath, requesting a tray in her room. Her distraught reflection in the mirror there seemed to taunt her. How many times had she sought her soul in a mirror during the years since she had met Alex? How many times had she asked herself why her life was in such turmoil?

The pain and the anxiety had always melted down to the same source. Love. Such a cruel emotion to the unlucky. It was love which was stalking her like Nemesis now. She had never managed to kill her love for Alex. She had dug the weakness down deep and sought to bury it, but it had lingered, preventing her from finding peace even with herself. When had loving Alex ever caused her anything but pain? She did not marvel at her own reluctance to admit her vulnerability. Pride and simple fear had warred against the admission.

'Sofia tells me that you are not feeling well.'

'It's just a headache. I'll lie down for an hour.' Her voice emerged perfectly normally and she turned.

Alex was on the threshold, dark and tawny and compellingly masculine. Concern showed clearly in his narrowed, probing scrutiny.

'Leave me, I'll be fine,' she insisted when he continued to stare.

'Are you in love with Steven Glenn?'

The unexpectedness of the quiet demand took her by surprise. His eyes were cool and level. The weather might have been under discussion.

'Why should you think that?'

His arrogant head tilted back, black hair gleaming in the filtered sunshine. 'I was curious, and it's wiser if we don't have any secrets between us.'

'You've got everything else, Alex,' she heard herself riposte drily. 'I'm afraid you don't have access to my every thought too.'

Fury glittered in his gaze. The illusion of cool was abruptly cast aside. 'Then you will understand if I prevent you from returning to England in the foreseeable future,' he delivered crushingly.

As he withdrew, the door rocked on its hinges. A sick tide of bitterness rose like bile within her. How could he think that she could love another man and still abandon herself to *him?* It certainly clarified Alex's view of her. As far as Alex was concerned, she was enslaved by her own promiscuous nature. Already he was suspecting his conviction that there had been no other men. He would have her watched like a thief when he was abroad. He would never trust her out of his sight. But she understood why he could live with her moral deficiency. It was her weakness, not his. Had his surveillance of her life included a photo of Steven? A humourless smile curved her lips. Steven was a very handsome man. Well, let Alex live with his suspicions! Steven was at a safe distance. If Alex had to distrust her, Steven was a harmless focus.

When she returned to the terrace after lunch, Alex was not there.

'Kyrios Veranchetti has gone fishing.' Sofia answered her enquiry cheerfully.

She got a pair of binoculars and located him out in the bay.

'He with old Andreas like when he was a boy,' Sofia burbled, sketching an impossibly miniature Alex with a workworn hand.

She could see two figures in the shabby *caique.* Sunlight glinted off a can of beer in Alex's hand.

She put the binoculars away guiltily and spent the afternoon sunbathing. He came back just before dinner, angling her a flashing, sensual smile on his way past. 'I won't take long to change.'

He talked with animation over the meal. Their earlier conversation might never have happened. As she went to bed, she was wondering how she was to survive another decade of Alex's supreme self-sufficiency. He didn't care if she loved another man. He had her in body, he didn't need her in spirit, too. She was almost asleep when he came to her. Her drowsy, muffled protest was silenced by the tender caress of his mouth. If he had been storm and passion the night before, he was seduction and silence now. But this time she was agonisingly conscious of his withdrawal afterwards. He quietly removed himself back to his own room. Actually sleeping with her appeared to be an intimacy Alex could not bring himself to contemplate.

She woke up to the sound of the helicopter landing. When she walked out on to the terrace Alex was chattering in Italian on the phone, and two dark-suited men, one standing, one sitting, were with him. Her colour evaporated as she recognised one of them. The older one with the greying hair was Roberto Carreras, the lawyer Alex had sent to Florence with the separation papers. Just looking at the man brought back hideous recollections.

'Some coffee, *kyrie?*' Sofia bustled past, carrying a laden tray, and the men turned their heads, seeing her slim figure for the first time. It was too late to retreat.

Carreras immediately stood, his suave features betraying not an ounce of discomfiture as he politely spun out his chair for her. '*Buon giorno, signora,*' he said, and passed some meaningless comment on the magnificent view.

She was ill with mortification, forced to take the seat and smile in the man's general direction. Alex glanced up, an abstracted half-smile softening his expression. Sofia moved about, pouring the coffee, pressing Kerry for a breakfast order. But if she ate, she would very likely throw up, she acknowledged. She had been so distressed that day. The lawyer had remained coldly impersonal while she had begged him to speak to Alex for her, had begged him to convince Alex that he had to come and see her face to face.'That is not my client's wish, *signora,*' he had intoned expressionlessly.

In restrospect, she marvelled that she had survived that period. A shudder of fearful repulsion snaked through her as she surveyed Alex from beneath her copper lashes. 'Excuse me.' She got up on cotton-wool legs with a slightly bowed head. 'I'll leave you to your business discussion.'

Strolling into the house, she could feel Alex's questioning glance burning into her back. She went out to the terrace at the rear of the villa. How could she sit and make polite conversation with a man who had witnessed and played a part in her humiliation? It was too much to demand of her. But Alex was an unfeeling, insensitive brute. He probably didn't even remember that Carreras was the one.

There were too many cracks to paper over. This marriage could never work. Even her innocence could not wipe out the memory of a nightmare. Yesterday she had let herself float with the tide because she loved him and she had wanted to cling to the fragile hope that he had meant it when he talked about a fresh start. What a fool she had been!

She was standing by the sea wall, gazing down

sightlessly at the waves crashing white foam against the rocks far below, when firm hands curved hard to her shoulders from behind. She flinched.

'They've gone,' Alex drawled roughly.

So he had remembered . . . my God, how could either of them ever forget?

'You've got to let me go, Alex,' she whispered. It was the only answer that she could see.

His fingers bit painfully into her slender forearms. 'No,' he gritted. 'Why should you talk like this now?'

'You're hurting me.'

His hold loosened, his thumbs rubbing soothingly over the indentations of his hard fingers. 'I didn't mean to. I think I have bruised you. Forgive me.'

An hysterical laugh bubbled up in her convulsed throat.

'I remembered too late to protect you from that embarrassment. It won't be repeated. It was an unfortunate oversight. You will not have to see him again.'

The laugh escaped this time, high-pitched and unnatural. 'What are you going to do? Tell him he's no longer welcome in your home because he once performed a certain task at your behest?'

'I will transfer him somewhere. He will not suffer by it. I can do no more. If you are so upset by the sight of him, I can no longer entertain him,' Alex retorted with abrasive practicality.

She gulped. 'I see. Are you planning to do that with everybody who might talk? The staff in the house in Florence, the security men, your secretarial staff in Rome who never put through my calls, the personal aides who ensured my letters were returned . . . what about the other lawyers involved?'

Spinning her round, he gave her a little shake.

Perspiration gleamed on his hewn dark skin, lines of strain grooved deep between his nose and mouth. 'Stop this now,' he insisted in a ragged undertone.

She turned up her tear-stained face in a movement of despair. 'You're not being logical, Alex. Athene may not descend to gossip, but a lot of your friends must be in the know. I know what a hotbed of gossip Roman society is, and the way rumours go, I should imagine that the word is that you walked into an orgy by now . . . ' She faltered out of all control and restraint. 'Doesn't it bother you that people are going to mutter and sneer behind your back?'

His hands sprung wide as he released her. He backed off several steps as if he could not trust himself too close. Slowly she shook her head, Titian hair flying about her in fiery glory. It had had to be said, all that Alex did not want to hear, for as those things happened she would be the one to pay the price.

'Don't you see that you will take your anger out on me?' she pressed hoarsely.

'*Cristo!*' The muscles in his strong brown throat worked. 'How can you believe that of me?'

Her arm steadied her weary body against the wall. 'You can't turn the clock back, Alex. You've got to see that. It was over for us a long time ago. You should have left me alone. You saw me in hospital and you acted on an ego-ridden whim. There is no going back. Let me go . . . '

He swung away from her, his brown hands clenching into impotent fists. She did not know whether his aggression was aimed at her for ripping the lid off the reality he ignored or aimed at all those faceless people who might dare to whisper. He punched one fist into his palm with a thud which tremored through the hot, still air. His golden gaze

struck sparks from hers in an uncompromising refusal
to yield.

'I believe I would sooner see you dead than let you
go. I want you too much, and I am not afraid of
gossip. Nor should you be, for who would dare to
insult you to your face?' he demanded fiercely. 'It will
be a brave man who dares to offend me. This is
between us and nobody else, don't you see that?'

'I can't take it, Alex,' she said in a stifled whisper. 'I
was content as I was.'

A black brow shot up. 'You will be content with me.
If you can accept me in bed, it is only a matter of time
before you accept me everywhere else.'

'Never! It's too late.' Hectic pink searing her
cheekbones at his blunt reminder of her weakness, she
tried to walk away. The intensity of the powerful
emotions simmering between them had exhausted
her. Alex would never admit to a wrong decision. He
would manoeuvre and manipulate and calculate to the
bitter end in an effort to make it a right one. But when
he talked of removing Carreras from the scene, he was
touching the tip of an iceberg, and evading the issue.
Carreras has only been an instrument, a highly paid
professional man doing his job. It was the man behind
the instrument who had driven her nearly crazy with
grief.

Only black storm clouds loomed ahead. Alex was
not omnipotent. He liked to think he was, though. He
had been born into wealth beyond most people's
wildest dreams. His Midas touch had transformed
wealth into legend. Her supposed infidelity was
probably the only situation that Alex had ever met
which was outside his control. She had offended in a
way no other living person would have dared to
offend. He still regarded her as his, indisputably his,

and no man and no woman could be permitted to take
what belonged to Alex before he chose to discard it. She
was the one slap in the teeth Alex had ever had, and with
masochistic fervour Alex was seeking to redress that slur
on his masculinity. How stupid she had been to believe
Nicky his main motivation in this marriage!

'I wish I could go back and change some of the
actions I took.' The harsh confession was dredged
from him. 'But even if I could, I do not believe I could
have behaved differently . . . '

An anguished smile twisted her pale face. How like
Alex it was to lament and negate in one savagely
candid statement.

'You were very young and I was hard, but I suffered
too,' he asserted roughly. 'On three separate occasions
I flew to Florence during those six months.'

She stilled and whirled jerkily back.

'Once I got as far as the gates of Casa del Fiore
before I told the driver to turn back.' The dark eyes
had no shimmer of gold. They were black and deep as
Hades. 'And you should be glad I turned back. I did
not trust myself near you.'

A picture of Alex flying into Florence and
backtracking in triplicate frankly astonished her. Her
imagination balked at the vision of Alex controlled by
rampant indecision. But that he had tried to make
himself approach her, that he had been drawn against
his own volition, softened the dead-weight of
resurrected bitterness which Roberto Carreras had
aroused. Instinctively she moved back towards him.
'W . . . What did you want to say?' Her voice was
almost inaudible.

His jawline clenched rock-hard. 'Why? Why, that is
what I wanted to say. Was it because he was younger
than I, better-looking, more exciting? Was it out of

badness or out of need?' he selected in a savage undertone which froze her in her tracks with a sudden onslaught of throat-constricting fear. 'Was he good? How often did he take you, how did he take you? That was all that was on my mind!'

His slim, beautifully shaped hands folded over the balustrade of the wall, the knuckles showing white. A surge of frightening anger had him in its merciless grasp. She was sentenced to appalled stillness by the horrific reality of how deeply Alex had been affected. She wanted to speak, she wanted to drag her sister kicking and screaming into his presence and wipe it all out. But common sense kept her quiet. In the mood Alex was in, the explanation would sound like fanciful nonsense. It would enrage him even more.

'And still sometimes it is on my mind. Because I never got my hands on him, and if I ever did I would kill him.'

She trembled. 'But . . . if you'd actually seen me, don't you think you might have had other . . . things to say?' she whispered.

'I knew you were not well. I was kept informed by your doctor. If I had come to you and you had lost our child, I could not have lived with myself.'

It was not an answer to her question. But it had been a sentimental question. At no stage had Alex seen the smallest hope of a reconciliation.

'And that day at the hospital, after Nicky's birth, I looked at you,' he breathed, 'and I hated you for what you had done to us both. I never wanted to look upon you again, but I could never put you behind me where you belonged.'

Was that what this marriage was aimed at achieving? Deep down, was that what Alex was really seeking? He had called her a fever in his blood. He

would secretly despise such a weakness in himself, but
he would not admit to it in self-denigrating terms. She
was suddenly convinced that, whether he appreciated
it or not, Alex was hoping to look at her with perfect
indifference at some time in the future.

'And you still believe we can make a new start?' she
queried.

His proud profile tautened. 'It is natural for us to
drag up all the feelings that we never shared then. By
doing so, we will lay them to rest.'

If more honest sessions akin to what she had just
undergone lay ahead, a quick, merciful dive off a cliff
would be kinder to her twanging emotions.

'I didn't deliberately seek to hurt you then.' Alex
looked down at the seas battering the rocks below and
emitted a harsh laugh. 'I was not really myself. If it
had been drugs, drink, illness . . . insanity, anything
but infidelity, I would have stood by you.'

He stepped away from the wall. 'Do not ask me to
let you go again. I don't like this view you have of
yourself as a prisoner,' he admitted. You have
everthing that any normal woman could want, and I
take very little in return.'

He was daring her to disagree. His anger had gone,
but he would have relished a good rousing battle to
blow off the cobwebs. When she thought about it, she
was the only person she had ever known who argued
with Alex. 'You take everything,' she contradicted
painfully, and this time she did manage to walk away.

It was lunch before they came together again. Alex
was back on the rails of cool, implacable good
humour. He suggested they spend the afternoon on
the beach and he wouldn't let her brood. 'You see,
you are not unhappy,' he stated with arrogant
emphasis the first time she laughed at one of his

sallies. 'You only think you are, and perhaps you want to be, but you are not.'

'Were you very unhappy when I left you in Florence?' he asked, with a naïveté which could only astound, in the depths of her bed that night.

His limbs were still damply entangled with hers, his breath warming her cheek. In itself, the question was a miniature breakthrough in intimacy. Alex was normally edging away by that stage, making her wonder melodramatically if he hated himself in the aftermath of their passion. It was also the first time that he had ever made a personal enquiry as to her state of mind then.

'Scared,' she muttered. 'Lonely.'

His lean body stiffened in the circle of her arms. His damp, silky hair brushed her brow as he lowered his head. 'For him?'

'Oh, go to hell, Alex!' After an outraged second of disbelief that he could even think that, she yanked herself violently free of him. 'How can you say that? I loved you, God, but I loved you!' She buried her contorted face in the pillows, her narrow back defensively presented to him.

'From love of so fine a strength, a man would surely take great comfort . . . ' he raked back at her in cruel cynicism. 'The love I got from you I bought. Your head was turned by my money and your body was ripe for a man's possession. Do not call that love!'

He slammed out of the room. Something went crashing noisily down in the corrridor and she heard a groaned profanity. He had hit himself on the small table she had put outside to carry a vase of flowers. She sincerely hoped it had hurt like hell. If he wanted to play musical beds in the middle of the night and throw right royal rages, he deserved everthing he got.

*   *   *

'I'm sorry . . . how often must I say it?' Alex thundered across the table at lunch time the next day. 'Yes, Alex, no, Alex, if you like, Alex! What kind of conversation is this?'

Sofia had almost dropped the coffee-pot. Out of the corner of her eye, Kerry noted her hasty retreat from the roar of Alex driven beyond endurance by silence. 'I can't get very chatty about the idea that I married you for money and sex,' she said bitterly. 'Somehow you have twisted up our whole relationship. I didn't cost you a groat in comparison with anybody else's ex-wife. You got off really cheap,' she pointed out coldly.

'I didn't want to get off cheap.'

'Of course you didn't! If I'd ripped off every penny I could get, you'd have loved it. It would have proved that I was grasping.' Breathing tempestuously, she settled back, wearing a baleful expression. She had hardly slept last night. She had been furious. On half a dozen occasions she had been tempted to wade into his room and bawl him out like a fishwife. Sorry wasn't always good enough.

'What do you want me to do? Get down on my knees?' he replied caustically.

'I'd kick you if you did, so I shouldn't bother,' she responded tartly, catching the disorientating twitch of his mouth. Her own anger dissipated rapidly. They were squabbling like a pair of children.

He drove his fingers through his black hair and studied her. 'Let's go for a walk,' he suggested ruefully.

Beyond the house, he dropped an arm round her tense shoulders. 'I lost my temper,' he sighed. 'And perhaps I lost it because what you said upset me.'

He turned her round and dropped a kiss on the crown of her head. His careless action had the most outsize effect upon her. It was the first gesture of affection he had shown in an entire week. Up until now he had only ever held her as a prelude to making love, and last night she had angrily decided that that would happen no more. Now she was swerving again. Could a physical relationship bring them close? The lack of one would certainly drive them apart. But she suffered from the insecure fear that she was simply adding to his low opinion of her. Would he have respected her more, would he have been more inclined to listen to her if she had found the will-power to deny them both that outlet?

'I wasn't a very attentive husband then, was I?' he mused when they were on their way back to the house. 'You must often have been lonely, even when we were living together. Why the hell didn't I go with you to that party in Venice?'

Her face shadowed.

'Shall I tell you why? It was so trivial. I was making a point. I was taking a stand. I worked late on into the evening, and then all of a sudden I got angry. I lifted the phone and ordered the jet to go on standby. I felt very self-righteous.'

'Don't . . . ' Should she try to explain? He seemed in an unusually quiet and approachable mood. As she hovered on the brink of an explanation that might well have proved momentous in the face of Alex's candour, someone came out of the house and waved.

'Spiros. The post must have come in,' Alex sighed. 'He remembers the workaholic I used to be.'

CHAPTER EIGHT

SOFIA had coffee waiting for them in the lounge. Alex, flicking through the envelopes, suddenly paused and strode over to her where she sat. 'For you,' he said.

He dropped the letter into her lap and she lifted it, recognising Steven's impossibly neat copperplate handwriting. She tucked the envelope in her pocket and collided with Alex's dark, intent scrutiny. She didn't realise what was wrong until he finally breathed, 'Aren't you going to read his letter?'

He had recognised the postmark, of course. 'Why, do you want to read it too?' she enquired in exasperation. 'Honestly, Alex, Steven is my friend and my partner, and he has never wanted to be anything else.'

'That has not been the impression I have received,' he parried icily.

She had had enough, and he had barely begun. If Alex was even going to question her mail, what hope did they have? Could adultery be committed on paper? He really would not be satisfied until he had her locked away in a little cage. Warding off the urge to leap down his throat, she murmured gently, 'You're going to have to learn to deal with your jealousy, Alex.'

Even as she said it, she could have bitten out her tongue. She might as well have dropped a burning rag on the surface of something highly inflammable.

He went up like a Roman candle. 'Jealousy?' he erupted in raw rejection. 'Of what would I be jealous?'

She paled. 'Maybe possessiveness should have been the word I used. I don't know. But I do know that there is a problem.'

'And shall I tell you what it is? My wife does not have male friends. Either you sell out your interest in the partnership or you give it to him. I don't care,' he grated. 'But you will sever the connection completely.'

For the second time he missed out on the coffee. Kerry wiped at her damp eyes. The illusion of greater understanding between them was destroyed. She no longer wondered why he had brought her to Kordos. The men in the village held Alex in the highest esteem. None of them would have dared eye up his wife. He owned the island, he was their benefactor. Whether Alex saw it in himself or not, he really wanted to wall her up alive and prevent her from coming into contact with other men. What hope did she have of combatting his distrust? Vickie, what did you do to us both? she questioned miserably.

She read Steven's letter. It was fortunate that Alex had not tried to do so. 'Feel like telling me the truth yet? Remember this shoulder is always here. I make a great wailing wall when I'm not wailing myself.' It chirped along much as Steven did, filled with personal questions, casual endearments and entreaties to write soon and tell him where she had hidden the spare keys for the MG. An impending visit from Barbara received a careless reference. 'I can't cope without you, seriously I can't,' he completed. 'Please dump him and come home.'

She sighed. No, he wouldn't be managing. He was too disorganised. As long as there was food on the table and petrol for the car, he would be happy. He had no ambition beyond that level, and he had depended on her heavily. If Barbara was half the woman Kerry thought she was, she would step into the breach. The business, properly run, would keep a married couple comfortably.

It was early evening when the call came. Spiros came into the lounge to have a discreet word with Alex. Kerry was lying on a couch reading an English newspaper and ignoring an atmosphere which postively pulsed with unspoken expectations. She had given Alex no reason to suspect Steven. The thought of lowering herself to further explanations stuck in her throat and a mention of Barbara now would probably strike Alex as highly suspicious.

'It seems you have a caller who refuses to identify himself.'

Her head flew up. 'I have a visitor here?' she said in amazement.

'A phone call,' Alex contradicted.

She began to get up, but Spiros was already passing her the nearest extension. She swept up the receiver, fully expecting to hear her sister's voice. The voice she did hear shot her in a state of imminent heart failure back on to the couch.

'Kerry? If it's you, for God's sake say something,' the New York twang implored. 'I'm not much good at cops and robbers.'

'It's me.'

'I guess you won't have forgotten me completely. Jeff Connors?'

Had Vickie got hold of him, after all? It seemed conscience had finally won out. Dazedly, Kerry was practically digging the phone into her ear in case the voice travelled within incendiary distance of Alex. To her intense relief, he sprang up and left the room.

'I'm alone now. You can talk,' she muttered.

'Vickie told me everything. You've got to believe me when I tell you that I had no idea you and your husband got a divorce. I just couldn't leave it lying so I came over. . . '

'Over where?' Her heartbeat had hit the Richter scale.

'Athens. I'm trying to rig transport over to this island of yours.'

'Are you crazy?' she hissed in disbelief. 'You can't come here, you mustn't come here. He'd kill you before you . . . '

'If your husband still feels that strongly, I was right to come.'

'Have you got a death wish?' she murmured, thinking in a hurry, which was difficult when she was in a complete panic. 'Don't come to the island. Wait until we get home to Florence and bring Vickie with you. That's essential.'

'So you do want the story told?'

'Yes, of course I do.' In her dumbfounded horror at the vision of Jeff stepping on to Kordos, she had not immediately picked up the significance of his willingness to redress the damage he had done. He really had to be a much nicer person than she had ever imagined if he was ready to take the trouble . . . not to mention the risk. Maybe he was just too stupid to realise what Alex was likely to do if he came across him. Alex would wipe him off the face of the earth before he even got his mouth open.

'We owe you and it will be straightened out,' he promised. 'I'll persuade Vickie by kidnapping if necessary. You see, I've got my own aspirations riding on this, too. I want to marry your sister.'

She came off the phone in shock. Vickie had told
her so many lies. But her silence in London was now
explained. She had been protecting Jeff. From Alex?
Or from the knowledge of her own behaviour? After
all, if Jeff, who existed in Kerry's memory as a lanky
blond man with formless features, was talking about
marrying her sister, his good opinion would not have
been something Vickie wished to risk losing. Clearly
they were very friendly and had obviously remained
in touch. Having told all to Kerry, Vickie had
evidently confessed to Jeff as well. Kerry shook her
buzzing head to clear it. It was like a chain reaction,
and if it kept on moving . . . dear lord, Kerry might
just have a marriage with a future again.

'That was Steven. His idea of a joke.' She lied
without a blush, popping her head round the door of
Alex's study with a wide smile.

He had a glass of whisky in his hand. His sombre
features merely tightened, but she ignored them. A
heady surge of hope was rising within her as she
adjusted to the import of the call she had received.
Alex could not deny both Jeff and Vickie, surely?
Even for Jeff to face him was a revealing fact within
itself. But it all had to be done properly. She sighed.
'Alex, please try to trust me.'

'How? Do I police you everywhere I go?' he
demanded scathingly. 'I almost lifted the phone to
listen to your call. To even think along such lines
unmans me!'

She drew in a long, sustaining breath. Had he been
less self-restrained she would probably have been
swandiving off the terrace right now and striking out
for the nearest patch of dry land. She inwardly
thanked her guardian angel for Alex's principles.
There was never anything sneaky about Alex in his

dealings with her . . . aside of that business with Willard Evans and all the prying he had done. But she was in a good enough mood to concede well-meant intentions on those counts. Really, there was always a bright side to be found if you looked hard enough. And Kerry was suddenly seeing bright sides all around her for the first time in years.

Over dinner, Alex's silence passed over her preoccupied head. When she went off to bed, she slept like a log. The last agonies of the long nightmare would soon be over, she reflected cheerfully when she awoke the next day.

'I'm glad to see you so happy,' Alex commented sardonically over breakfast.

Her nose wrinkled as she tasted her coffee. It had a curious sharp flavour, but Alex didn't appear to be finding anything amiss with his. She munched a piece of fruit to freshen her mouth. 'Are we leaving for Florence soon?'

Dark eyes swept her unwittingly hopeful face. His thick lashes screened his gaze. 'No. I am content here for the moment.'

'You said a week, maybe two,' she reminded him. 'I miss Nicky.'

'He can always come out here to join us.' He shrugged with cool finality. 'If you want to do some shopping, I'll take you to Athens.'

'I do occasionally take my mind out of my wardrobe.'

'And where does it travel then?' he murmured with a satiric edge.

Slowly she counted to ten. She still got up. 'I feel like some fresh air. I'll go down to the beach for a walk.'

'Don't go far. Carina and Ricky will be here for

lunch,' he warned her. 'They're leaving for New York tomorrow. He's taking charge of our public relations department over there.'

She managed a smile at the news. She liked Carina the best of Alex's sisters, but her mind was more intent on how speedily she could bring Alex and Vickie and Jeff together in Florence. Jeff had said that he would fly back to London today. Impatience shrilled through her as she went down the steep steps to the beach. She was terrified that Jeff would lose interest or that Vickie would persuade him against his plan. If he was in love with her, Vickie would have influence over him. Perhaps in the heat of the moment Jeff had flown out to Greece. Kerry had stopped him in his enthusiastic tracks. Suppose he gave up the idea? Vickie wanted to pretend that it was all in the past. She was afraid to face Alex. Her pride revolted against the concept.

Kerry wandered along the rocky beach, the sun beating down on her in golden warmth. She had been walking for some time when she came on the small cove where a yacht was moored. A bunch of sun-tanned young people were strewn out on the sand, sunbathing, while a stereo cassette pounded out Bruce Springsteen.

'You can't be a local!' A dark-haired youth proclaimed loudly. 'Not with that gorgeous hair. I refuse to believe it.'

She grinned. 'You're English.'

Within five minutes she was sitting down with the group. There were two couples and one odd man out. They had rented out the small, shabby yacht to do a tour of the islands, and they were lively company.

'The people in the village aren't too friendly,' Hilary, the curvaceous blonde complained. 'We got flung out of the taverna last night because Dave got on the wrong side of one of the men. We got all this guff about this being a private island, and the local cop saw us off at the harbour so we simply shifted anchor. Are you staying at the taverna?'

Kerry was reluctant to admit who she was, for they had accepted her as one of them. She was enjoying the sound of her own language and the easiness of her welcome. 'No, I'm staying at a private house. With my husband,' she added circumspectly.

'You're married?' Dave, the one who had originally spoken to her, groaned in mock despair.

She laughed. 'I've got a son of almost four.'

'He must have stolen you out of the cradle. Rather you than me,' the other girl, Ann, said feelingly. 'Life's too short to get tied up young.'

'It depends on the man,' Kerry murmured, unperturbed, and the conversation moved on to the places they had been and where they were hoping to get before their restricted budget ran out.

'I'm gasping for a cold drink.' Hilary gave her boyfriend a nudge in the ribs. 'Go on, take a walk into the village. The shop's right on the edge of it.'

In the end, two of the men went off. Kerry sat, cross-legged, talking about Antiques Fayre with Hilary, suppressing her regretful awareness that she was really describing a closed chapter in her life. Ann decided she was hungry and swam out to the yacht. Kerry rested back on the sand, letting the sun wash her upturned face and extended legs.

She must have dozed off for the next thing she knew, somebody was tugging playfully at her hair. Her eyes opened. Dave was bending over her, too close for comfort. 'Where is everybody?'

'I persuaded Hilary to push off.'

'Why?' she asked baldly, glancing simultaneously down at her watch. 'Oh no . . . ' she groaned.

He caught her arm and prevented her from scrambling up. 'Oh, come on, you can't be leaving. You came down here for a bit of company, didn't you, and I'm more than willing to play ball,' he told her with a thick, suggestive smile. 'We could go somewhere a little quieter.'

'Are you crazy?' Kerry snapped, her pleasure in the little friendly interlude now destroyed by Hilary's desertion and Dave's phenomenal conceit. The nerve of him, she wasn't looking for a toy boy!

Before she could pull free of him, his weight pinioned her down as his hand thrust at her shoulder and he made a rough, clumsy effort to kiss her. In sudden, frank fear, for he was considerably bigger and heavier than she was, she was trying to raise her knee when Dave went flying from her in a blur of movement. As he hit the ground several feet away, she pulled herself upright automatically, a gasp of stricken horror on her lips as she saw Alex dragging the winded Dave up with one powerful hand. Her husband's dark face was a mask of murderous fury. As his fist connected in a sickening thud of flesh on bone, she screamed, 'Alex . . . stop it!'

All her life she had shrunk from violence. She wanted to end the carnage, but her feet were rooted to the spot by paralysed fear. The third time Alex hit him, the suffocating blackness folded in on her. She crumpled down on the sand as if he had struck her.

When she came out of the faint, she was lying on her bed and a whole row of faces were around her. 'That boy . . . oh, my God,' she mumbled as it all came back to her in a wave.

Someone's hand gripped hers. Somewhere at a distance Alex was speaking in a vituperative and vicious spate of Italian. 'He's all right, Kerry.' It was her sister-in-law's voice. 'Ricky stopped Alex in time.'

'I thought he was going to kill him . . . '

Carina came down on the edge of the bed, shooing off the female staff with sharp orders. The room cleared. She turned over the cool cloth on Kerry's brow. Kerry still couldn't stop shaking. She kept on seeing Alex wreaking havoc on an over-amorous youth barely out of his teens. Abruptly, she clutched Carina's hand. 'You've got to get me away from here . . .' she muttered in despair.

'What is happening between Alex and you?' Carina was pale and concerned. 'A young man tries to kiss you on the beach and Alex goes out of his head. I never saw him lose control before, but my brother would not harm you.'

Kerry looked at her with desolation in her empty eyes. She was defeated for the last time. Alex had broken every bond he held her by. Her emotions had gone into the cold storage of shock. All she could feel was a tearing, desperate need to escape his domination. She didn't care any more about Jeff and Vickie and her airy-fairy hopes of their marriage surviving. It was a brief dream sequence she no longer had the heart to contemplate.

'We were walking along the shore to find you,' Carina related. 'You always forget the time. But Alex was laughing, you know . . . he was not annoyed . . . '

'I wish he had hit *me*.' Kerry was not even listening to her.

'How can you say that? Alex would never touch you. He thought you were being assaulted. Any man would have . . . no,' Carina sighed unhappily. 'It was not right what he did. We saw one thing. He saw another. We saw the girl swim out towards the boat.

It was obvious that there was nothing questionable.
But Alex . . . Alex is crazy jealous of you.'

Kerry was enveloped in her own despair. She didn't
hear Alex come in, but his wrathful, 'Who are you to
keep me from my wife?' penetrated. She shifted away
in automatic recoil. She couldn't even bring herself to
look at him.

'You animal,' she whispered, unable to silence the
reaction.

His flushed complexion lost colour.

She realised that he wouldn't leave her alone
without an explanation. Woodenly, resentfully, she
summed up a brief hour spent chatting to some young
holidaymakers. It was punctuated and interposed by
Alex's imprecations.

'Ah . . . you start talking to strangers, not even
strangers from your own background,' Alex gritted.
'Cheap tourists. Perhaps you forget who you are. You
don't belong with such people.'

No, it was Alex she did not belong with. Once he
had been a stranger. He would have remained one had
she not possessed a bright, outgoing personality and
the thick-skinned bravado of a friendly teenager. 'I
spoke to you in a lift,' she murmured helplessly.

To her surprise, he was quick to grasp the
connection. 'That was different.'

No, it hadn't been different. She had always talked
to people around her. She had always liked meeting
new friends. Alex had been attracted by her vivacity,
but he had caged her for the same trait. He chose to
forget too that those cheap tourists came from a
background of greater prosperity than her own.

'Is that how you met? In a lift?' Much intrigued,
Carina was eager to lighten the brooding atmosphere.

Kerry's eyes were wry. 'He practically cut me dead.'

'*Per dio* . . . ' Alex raked. 'You go back six years to complain!'

She had still to look at him, though she didn't need to look. His lean, strikingly handsome features were permanently inside her head.

'I'll leave you alone.' Carina escaped uncomfortably.

As the door shut, Alex planted himself where she could no longer avoid visual contact. 'What is the matter with you? ' Hmm?' he demanded, dulled golden eyes pinned to her in derision. 'You were flirting. How else did you get into the situation? They didn't even know who you were. My wife does not mix with people who trespass on private property. Have you no sense of propriety? No sense of discretion? Must I have you watched every place you go?'

Every harsh word lashed into her. She had no answers for him. A thick, impenetrable wall of glass separated them in understanding. She was only twenty-three years old, and just over a year of that time had been spent in the goldfish bowl of Alex's elitist society. But Alex had never granted her trust. She recognised how he had confined her with his family and vetted everyone she met. Her only escape route had been through Vickie. Alex had subconsciously behaved from the outset as if her betrayal was written into the stars. Somehow it helped to see that his excessive possessiveness had existed even then without just cause. She was not responsible for its birth.

'I want to leave with Ricky and Carina,' was all she said.

Their relationship was impossible. The poison of distrust and jealousy infiltrated every corner of Alex's mind. A flirtatious glance, a little animated chatter with a man anywhere between twenty and fifty and Alex would be suspicious. It would only get worse. He would imprison her and suffocate her until only enmity and resentment lay between them.

'No!' Alex seethed on another feverish blaze of anger.

It hurt that she should know exactly what he was thinking. He was incredulously reacting to the news that he was in the doghouse when he had only done what any Greek husband would have done to a man making advances to his wife. He was furious that she had not made a more detailed explanation. He was outraged that she was not ashamed of herself. And at the back of it all, he honestly believed that she had encouraged Dave. That was riling him too. He had punished the perpetrator, but not the instigator. His own code wouldn't let lay him lay violent hands upon a woman. But for how long could that restraint hold out?

She slept for a while, her own constant lassitude nudging and not quite connecting with some nebulous recollection. Carina was there again when she woke up. 'I'm staying for a few days,' she announced.

Kerry sat up. 'But you're supposed to be going to New York tonight,' she objected.

Carina smiled. 'Ricky can survive on his own for a few days. It's a service apartment and he'll be working all the time.'

'You don't need to stay.'

'Alex asked me to,' she revealed reluctantly. 'He's worried about you.'

'He wants to make sure that you join me on my next walk along the beach, I suppose,' Kerry gathered with bitter distaste.

'No, of course he doesn't.' Carina pressed her hand in reproof. 'He feels that you need a woman's company. Do you feel like dinner?'

She nodded. 'Where's Alex?'

'Down in the taverna, getting drunk,' Carina flushed. 'Ricky left him there. You were shocked by what he did. Don't you understand how upset he is?'

Kerry's face shuttered as she got off the bed, keen to have a bath and a change of clothes. 'It's not remorse, I'm sure. How was Dave?'

'He was all right,' Carina repeated, a tinge of disapproval in her tone. It was heartless of Kerry to enquire a second time about her amorous asailant when her husband was drinking himself into oblivion down in the village. 'His friends took him away. They were not decent young people, Kerry. That same young man insulted a fisherman's daughter in the village last night and started a fight.' Gathering steam, she looked up. 'And two girls and three men on a boat, none of them married. This speaks for itself. You are too trusting, Kerry.'

In the privacy of the bathroom, Kerry appreciated how a few hours of grace had altered Carina's views. She could not see fault in Alex for long. Thus she had reduced Alex's violence by making the tourists into promiscuous troublemakers. Kerry was no doubt in the wrong for speaking to them at all, and excused for her over-familiarity by a gullible nature. Or were Carina's suspicions running parallel with Alex's now that her brother had done something so appallingly uncharacteristic as hitting the bottle?

He had to let her go now for both their sakes. On that beach, she had seen her naïve hopes for the future shattered by hard reality. Even if Vickie and Jeff did approach him, she seriously doubted that Alex would

even give them a hearing. The poison had got too
deep a hold in four years apart.

'Do . . . do you love Alex?' Carina blurted out over
dinner, her plump face primed for a snub.

'Love's not always enough,' she answered heavily.
'He doesn't love me, but he has to keep me to prove
something to himself. Letting go would be as healthy
for him as it would be for me. We can't live in the past
now.'

It was too deep for Carina. She chewed her lower
lip. 'How can you talk about leaving him? You are
only newly married again. Alex was happy when we
arrived. Why are you so hard on him?'

Much later, Kerry turned over in her bed, and her
lashes flickered up on the dark silhouette of the figure
sunk in an armchair in the corner of the room. 'A . . .
Alex? Good lord, what time is it?' she whispered,
shaken by his silent presence.

'Does it matter?'

She rested back again, shrouded by the same numb
depression. 'No.'

'You should not be afraid of me,' he breathed
harshly. 'Earlier you behaved with me as if I was . . .
Cristo!' He sprang upright fluidly, his eyes glittering
in the moonlight as he emerged from the shadows.
'You are my wife, you are the mother of my child . . .
what happened today? It was not my fault. For that to
occur again—to see you with another man—naturally I
lost my temper.'

'Some day you might do it with me . . . '

'No!' He roared it at her in fierce rebuttal.
'Whatever you did, I would not touch you. I am not a
violent man.'

But his passions were. They ran at gale-force

turbulence with her. Everywhere else in Alex's life control and restraint ruled the roost. He was punctual, tidy, organised, immaculate in appearance. He carried enormous responsibility. He was a rock for his dependent and less able brothers and sisters to lean upon. He was in every other field a strong, principled and honourable man, worthy of respect. She was the fatal flaw that rocked Alex dangerously off balance.

'You've got to let me go,' she repeated wretchedly.

The mattress gave under his weight. He leant over her. 'These are teething problems. You are over-sensitive. All you can think about is running away. I do not run away from trouble. I face it,' he said hardily. 'And you will face it with me.'

'We're poison for each other.'

'Dio, such melodrama!' he growled. 'And stop lying there as if I am about to attack you!'

Helplessly, she turned her head away. It was a mistake. His fingers laced into her hair and his mouth covered hers in hungry retribution. He found no answer in her. She was as inanimate and as empty as a waxen doll. He flung his dark head back, his ruptured breathing pattern breaking the stillness. 'You can never be there for me when I need you,' he condemned raggedly. 'Why should I curse myself with a wife who has no love for me? Forgive me for forgetting that you are only here on sufferance. I will not disturb you again.'

She knew then that the same process was working within him. Alienation. It would only be a matter of time before Alex let her go. He was too proud to hang on to a wife who could not respond to him in bed. It was the ultimate offence, and what a pity it was that she had not contrived the miracle sooner. Since she was seeing the hope of freedom again, she could not understand why tears should wet her cheek and why she should ache at Alex's roughened belief that she turned her back on him when he most needed her. He had never talked about needing her before. Why did he have to talk about it now?

Three days later, she was uncompromisingly sick the instant she got out of bed. One of the maids heard her retching in the bathroom and fetched Sofia. Sofia arrived to beam meaningfully at her while she clung to the sink, trying to subdue a second debilitating bout of nausea. Her pinched face had a greenish pallor and her eyes were haunted. She had woken up feeling sick, the last two mornings. She hadn't wanted to think about the fact. She had suppressed the awareness that there had been no comforting physical proof as yet that she was not pregnant.

Oh, God, please, no, was all she could think now. They were leaving for Rome this morning. Alex had been distant and civil for the past forty-eight hours. All the portents were that he was withdrawing from her, slowly but surely, with the rigid control of a reformed addict staving off the need for another fix. Steeling herself to kill Sofia's hopeful smile, she said, 'Is there something wrong?'

The housekeeper frowned. 'Is the *Kyrie* ill?'

'I don't think last night's fish agreed with me. I've been feeling unwell all night.' Kerry tilted her chin.

Sofia retreated. Kerry splashed her face with unsteady hands. It couldn't happen, it just couldn't happen now. Her system could be upset by travel, the change in climate, the alteration in diet . . . by sheer nerves. But that night in London was all she could think about. One reckless night at the wrong time. The nausea, the dizziness and the lassitude were all horribly familiar. Alex had impregnated her and she wanted to scream blue murder. It wasn't fair, it just wasn't fair when she was already practically at her last gasp.

'Are you feeling well?' Carina enquired over breakfast. 'You seem very pale.'

'I had a restless night.' She studied the table. She felt like a plague carrier. She felt as if someone had painted a cross on her forehead. She was too self-conscious, too petrified to look anywhere near Alex. But in another sense she wanted to rage at him for his rotten potency. All she could think about was the horrendous misery of her months carrying Nicky, memories inextricably interwoven with what had been going on in her life simultaneously. The mere threat of repetition bereft her of all rationality, and if he found out he would never let her go.

How she got through the helicopter trip she never knew afterwards. It was mind over matter. She had suffered dreadfully from travel sickness, even in a car, when she was pregnant with Nicky. But air travel was the worst of all. On the flight to Rome, mind over matter was no longer sufficient to subdue the churning in her stomach. She spent most of the flight in the washroom, or so it seemed. Concealment had become impossible.

Carina hovered, muttering worriedly about food poisoning. Alex was pale and suspiciously silent after the receipt of one single glance of burning reproach from Kerry. The whole event might have been masterminded by fate to reveal her secret. The only time Alex had ever seen her airsick she had been pregnant. It did not take a lightning bolt of amazing perception for him to suspect the cause.

He insisted on carrying her off the plane. He had

recovered his colour, but he looked guilty as hell. It gave her a malicious pleasure that he should understand exactly how she felt. A doctor was waiting for her at the townhouse. Carina helped her into bed. By then, the penny had dropped with her, too.

'I was never like this. No wonder you are miserable,' she soothed sympathetically. 'It is very hard to be pleased when you feel so ill.'

'One swallow does not make a summer,' said the doctor glibly. 'No pregnancy is a blueprint of another. There may well be small similarities, but with rest and calm you could enjoy excellent health this time.'

Kerry saw nothing but misery ahead. As soon as he had gone and Alex's sisters and Athene had given up offering advice, she turned over in bed and wept inconsolably. The axe had fallen. Her body wasn't her own any more. How easy it was for the uninitiated to talk about the redeeming joys of motherhood when they did not have eight months of purgatory stretching in front of them, and a marriage that had already stopped being a marriage beforehand.

CHAPTER NINE

'THE doctor wants you to stay in bed for a few days.'

Kerry emerged from beneath her hair. 'I hate you!' she screamed.

Alex's black hair was ruffled, his tie was loose and his strain was palpable. She went back under her hair again, racked by the cruel injustice of it all. He didn't love her, she was going to be dumped in Florence again and left to suffer well out of Alex's radius. That doctor didn't know what he was talking about when he told her that things would be different this time around.

'You realise—you *must* realise that I cannot agree to an abortion,' Alex delivered, knotting the rope, did he but know it, round his own throat. 'I . . . I couldn't live with that. I wish I could, but I couldn't. Perhaps it will be a false alarm.' He sounded very much as if he hoped it was.

What sort of man was he to even think of such a solution? Horror darted through her in wrathful rejection. But desperate straits demanded desperate measures, she decided. When Alex was adapting to a strategic retreat from the battlefield of their marriage, fate had sprung a rear attack on him. Once again he was being condemned to fatherhood with a woman he didn't love, couldn't respect and couldn't live with.

'I'll never forgive you for even mentioning the possibility,' she mumbled feverishly. 'How could you even think about it for a moment? How could you

153

even say that?'

'I?' Alex unleashed, suddenly springing free of his unusually quiet manner and doing so loudly enough to make her look up in dismay. 'I . . . ' He pointed to himself in raw, flaring Latinate emphasis. 'Not want my own child? *Dio*, I am jubilant!' He slung the assurance at her, stressing each syllable so that the words rolled off his tongue in fluid provocation. 'And I'm not about to apologise for it, either. This time I will be able to watch my child grow. This time I will not be on the outside!'

It was eleven that evening before Alex reappeared. Having run the gamut of her emotions and vaguely appreciated that, no matter what stance Alex took, she would still be unreasonable, she was very quiet.

'I am taking time off to see that you look after yourself,' he announced aggressively in the darkness. 'If I could suffer for you I would, but I can't. I just don't want you to think that I am leaving you alone.'

He gathered her resistant body close with determined hands. His fingers spread protectively over her flat stomach in a movement which was uniquely revealing. 'How soon will we know?' he prompted impatiently.

He was holding her, at last he was simply holding her. But the baby had inspired the warm attitude of concern. He really was pleased, she realised. He had switched his possessiveness from her to the life inside her womb. So might he have patted an incubator. All of a sudden, everything else took second place. She sniffed. The numbness had faded again. Of course it had. Loving Alex was a life sentence. It really didn't matter what he did. It would always be the same.

Over the next three days he drove her scatty. She was deluged with fancy nightwear and the latest books, and adjured not a move a muscle. He seemed to be stocking her up to spend the next twenty years flat on her back. One of his sisters did him the cruel disservice of presenting him with a book on pregnancy. By the time Alex emerged, much stricken from its overly informative depths, a headache would have had him rushing her to the nearest hospital.

'Are you dying?' Nicky whispered from under her arm one afternoon. 'I heard *Nonna* say Daddy thought you were dying?'

He rocked her with laughter. He made her see the funny aspect to Alex's over-zealous attitude. When the doctor called, she asked him to speak to Alex. Otherwise Alex was never going to believe that she was fit to travel to Florence.

It was an hour before Alex appeared. 'You don't look healthy to me. Have I been making a fuss?' he prompted tautly.

It was her fault he had been, she acknowledged guiltily. How many times had she referred to previous sufferings? Had that been to punish him for his absence then? She did not like the picture. He was sincerely worried about the baby, and she was not an invalid.

'I think the doctor was right. It's not going to be as it was before, and even then there was no danger of a miscarriage,' she pointed out.

Alex stiffened. 'Why does it have to be like this?' he drawled in weary bitterness. 'All I ask of you is that you have this baby and love it, even though it is my child.'

She blinked back stinging tears. 'You don't have to say that to me, Alex. Don't you understand? I panicked, my nerves probably made me feel sick!'

she teased shakily. 'You don't have to feel . . . '

'Guilty?' His eyes were dark and sombre. 'I took no care of you that night. I thought only of my own needs. This did not need to happen.'

She frowned, cursing the childish recriminations she had hurled. 'Alex, I'm an adult too. I didn't think either, and it's not . . . it doesn't have to be a disaster. We both want this baby, don't you see? That's something we can share.'

His ebony brows pleated. 'It will be all that we share. We will live separately in the same household. That is what you wanted from the very beginning. It was unreasonable of me to demand anything else.'

Shot from shock to the unalterable discovery that what she had once believed she wanted was now as far removed from her present feelings as Alex appeared to be, she searched his face dazedly. 'Unreasonable?'

'Yes, it was. You saw more clearly than I. We must hope that we make better friends than lovers,' he quipped smoothly. 'It will certainly be less explosive.'

Her fingers knotted into the sheets. 'Friends?' she parroted to herself.

Alex vented a humourless laugh. 'I see the prospect confounds you, but why not? How else may we live together peacefully? When I forced you to marry me, I asked the impossible from us both. I have accepted that.'

'Yes.' She saw that he had reached that acceptance. He had dug down to the roots of his desire for her and exorcised it. If he no longer viewed her as a sexually attractive woman, he could banish his jealousy. Friends. Her mind boggled. She didn't want Alex as a friend, she couldn't suddenly switch off now. It was too late.

He smiled at her ruefully. 'So you see, there will be

be no further distressing scenes between us. I feel a lot happier knowing that.'

It was just as well somebody was in the mood to celebrate. Kerry wasn't. Didn't he see that those days on Kordos had been a necessary period of adjustment? Before that ghastly scene on the beach had erupted, a new and fragile understanding had been under formation, in spite of his jealousy. His behaviour had shattered her that day, and perhaps, she grasped now, it had shattered him too. He was really acting quite predictably. He saw a fault in himself. He rooted it out. After all, she might be the cause of the fault, but he was truly stuck with her now. Alex had brought logic to bear on their problems, and Alex's cool logic had never been less welcome.

Apart from a little nausea during the flight to Pisa airport, she was fine. The closer they got to journey's end, however, the more tense she became. Casa del Fiore had been her prison during their separation. She associated the eighteenth-century villa with unhappy memories. But evidently sentimentality had no such hold upon Alex.

The house was on the outskirts of Florence, set in the lush, rolling hills of the Tuscan countryside, which was already blossoming with the softening green veil of spring. The day they had viewed Casa del Fiore, it had been surrounded by an overgrown meadow of wild flowers, its dulled and neglected façade gleaming a faint pink in the dying sunlight. After the agent had gone, Alex had tumbled her down and made love to her among those flowers. She reddened and paled again with self-loathing. Memory looked like being her sole comfort. He had got tired of her even before that fight, she was convinced of it.

When had Alex ever denied himself anything he still wanted?

'Welcome home,' he murmured as the limousine swung between the tall, eagle-topped pillars at the foot of the long driveway.

Casa del Fiore seemed to drowse in the blaze of the noonday heat, the soft yellow walls of the rambling villa complemented by the terracotta roof tiles. The arrow-shaped cypresses lining the avenue cast thin shadows in the car's path.

She had chosen this house, not Alex. Her enthusiasm had been undiminished by the mountain of improvements required inside and out, and Alex had let her have her way. She had flung herself into transforming the drab interior, struggling with Italian workmen brought up to *'Domani'* and forever going over her head to talk to Alex, who had never had the time or the interest to deal with them. When he had left, she had stopped decorating, leaving only a few rooms complete.

Nicky scrambled out of the car first, eager to explore. Alex had never brought him here. He had closed the house up with only a caretaker. The staff were all new, smilingly grouped in the front hall. The ghastly cherry-red carpet she had mistakenly chosen for the floor still darkened the entrance.

Lucrezia, the housekeeper, beamed at her cheerfully and, as soon as the introductions were over, Kerry forgot about Alex and went off to explore. It was like moving into a timeslip. Everything was exactly as she had left it. The kitchens were still untiled. The rooms she hadn't touched were still empty and shuttered. An incredible medley of styles reigned supreme wherever her immature taste had lingered. The rear sitting-room still rejoiced in lamentably quarrelsome floral fabrics.

'I gather you didn't use the house at all,' she remarked, hearing his step behind her. 'It's pretty hard on the eye, isn't it?'

'I like it. It's bright, warm,' he replied almost abruptly.

Upstairs, her throat closed over in the doorway of their bedroom. For once her efforts for a cohesive scheme had come together. But the pale lemon-washed walls, the abundance of gorgeous fabric at the windows and over the bed made her turn away. How could he bring her back here? Didn't he have any sensitivity at all? Everywhere she looked she saw a frail, drooping shadow of herself in the past. Welcome home, indeed!

Brown fingers linked slowly with hers. 'Was it a mistake to bring you back? You loved this house.'

Irritably she rammed back her own eerie spectres. Alex suffered from no such imaginative qualms. 'Where will we put Nicky?' she asked, walking down the wide, sunlit corridor to glance into empty rooms. She had only furnished one guest-room. He hadn't changed that, either.

'I'll use the dressing-room off our bedroom,' he replied as if he could read her mind.

She gave a brisk nod, colour rising to her cheeks. Project one was evidently to furnish the room through the communicating door for Alex's occupancy. 'I've got a lot to do,' she mused.

'You mustn't overtire yourself,' he ruled. 'I will be here. Ask me to help with anything you wish.'

Unexpectedly, she laughed. 'Alex, the last time I showed you a wallpaper book, you spread a file on top of it.'

'I must often have hurt your feelings,' he remarked with unsmiling gravity. 'It won't be like that again.'

'I'm not expecting you to immerse yourself in household trivia,' she said dully, recoiling from his sacrificial attitude.

Later she watched him from the bedroom window. Nicky was kicking a ball towards him and throwing a short-tempered fit when Alex kicked it back past him. Shorn of his jacket and tie, his black hair tousled by the breeze, he looked remarkably relaxed as he scooped his son up and hugged him with an unashamed affection which jerked her own heartstrings with envy. He looked happy. He had put a wall between them that she didn't want, and he looked happy. He had only battled with his pride when he decided that they should opt for a platonic marriage.

When she was in bed, she thought of him lying in the narrow confinement of the single just through the wall while she tossed in more space than she could find comfort in. You'd better get used to it, she thought, Alex never changes his mind about a decision.

When she slept, she dreamt that she was locked inside a house without windows or doors. Everywhere she ran in her frantic need to escape she came on another stretch of blank wall. Her eyes flew open, a sob on her lips. Alex was bending over her. 'It's only a dream . . . hmm?' he soothed, and the fear went out of her. 'Do you want me to bring you a drink?'

Drowsily, she shook her head. She bit her lip, and then said it anyway, 'Don't go . . . '

Alex stilled at the foot of the bed, already in the act of leaving her. Stark embarrassment flooded her as she registered his surprise and reluctance. But the slither of his silk robe marked his agreement. 'Go back to sleep,' he murmured as he slid quietly into the other side of the bed.

When morning came, his head was against her shoulder, his thick hair brushing her chin, his arm lying heavily over the swell of her breasts. A mixture of hunger and tenderness gripped her as his dark lashes lifted and she merged with slumbrous gold. Immediately, he shifted away from her warmth. 'I don't think sharing a bed is a very good idea,' he murmured sardonically. 'The next time something goes bump in the night, I shall leave a light on for you.'

She forced a laugh and watched him depart, but she was stung to the quick, almost certain that he had seen the helpless invitation in her eyes. Her energies, it seemed, would be pinned more rewardingly to the house. Alex no longer found her an unbearable temptation.

The next few weeks were both tranquil and busy. She had the hall carpet lifted to reveal the beautiful pale pink Gavorrano marble beneath, and she engaged an interior designer. Alex was talking about setting up a branch of Veranchetti Industries in Florence and shifting his staff from Rome. She was astonished, but gradually came to appreciate that the concession was in keeping with an Alex determinedly taking an interest in every detail of the household upheaval and prowling round baby boutiques in her wake. At every opportunity Alex was proving that she could have no cause to complain of neglect. His enthusiasm and his good humour were daunting, but then he never did anything by halves, and, had his efforts to please led him into her bedroom, she could have been ecstatic. Unfortunately, Superhusband went to his own bed every night, and did not appear to be finding it a strain.

They came home from a shopping expedition in Florence one afternoon and there was another letter from Steven awaiting her. Alex passed it to her with a brilliant smile. 'He likes to keep in touch, doesn't he?' he quipped. 'Perhaps you will want him to visit with us this summer.'

Leaving her pole-axed, he strode off into the library. Had it been her imagination that he was jealous of Steven? What a lowering admission it was that the hint of a dark, brooding scowl from Alex on the subject of Steven would have made her day!

The same post included a letter from her mother, who wrote that she was rather concerned about Vickie. She had not been home since Kerry's departure. 'She's very strained over the phone, not like herself at all,' Ellen wrote. 'Do you think there's a man involved? I hoped that she might have confided in you.'

Kerry hadn't heard from Vickie, nor did she expect to. She assumed that Jeff's appeal to her sister had failed, and that with it his desire to unlock the past had waned. It was now almost four weeks since he had called her from Athens. Sooner or later, she would have to write to Vickie. She didn't want their parents upset by the discovery that their daughters were mysteriously at loggerheads. But it was still too soon for Kerry to face penning that letter. Her anger had subsided, and much of her bitterness, but she was still paying the price of that morning through her marriage.

The following morning, Lucrezia brought her breakfast in bed. Alex came in with Nicky, her son bouncing up and down with exuberant excitement. Still half asleep, she surveyed them.

'It's your birthday,' Alex said drily.

She blinked, for she had completely forgotten. 'Happy birthday!' Nicky cried, thrusting an envelope on top of her cup of tea and settling a luridly coloured box beside it.

'Happy birthday.' Alex pressed cool lips to her flushed cheek and presented her with a card. It was all very restrained and polite.

His card was one of those ones with no message. Admittedly, he would have had to sack Florence to find a card with a blurb suitable to their association. What it did have, though, was an enormous key taped inside.

Kerry looked at him hopefully. The key to the communicating door their between bedrooms, she thought wildly, for the lock was empty on both sides.

'It's a surprise,' he proffered with an oddly tense smile. 'We need to go out to fit the key to a door.'

Disgraced by her own imagination, she nodded. Eating breakfast was impossible after that. Nicky was left at home and Alex drove them into Florence. He parked by the Arno and took her walking through the narrow, crowded streets.

'Am I going to like it . . . the surprise?' she prompted doubtfully.

'I hope so . . . I think so.' The cool, sensual mouth curved into an almost boyish smile as he guided her off the Via Tornebuoni. 'I thought of it in Greece.'

He had been thinking of her birthday that far back? She could only be complimented. He grabbed her hand impatiently. 'Close your eyes,' he instructed, and his arm folded round her to move her on another few steps before turning her round. 'Now you can open them.'

'Am I supposed to see something?' she muttered, gazing at the green and gold decorated windows of the apparently empty shop in front of them.

He sighed. 'Look up to the name.'

What she read in flowing gold script immobilised her. Antiques Fayre—Firenze. While Alex employed the key in the door she tried to crank her jaw shut. Alex had bought her a shop?

'Aren't you coming in?'

She stood inside the enormous interior on the dusty floor which was littered with packing cases and rubbish. It was easily four times the size of what she had left behind. 'How . . . how did you get it? It's so central. It must have cost a fortune . . . or is it rented?'

Alex looked pained. 'It belongs to you. I made the previous owner an offer that he could not refuse. At the price, he might have removed the rubbish,' he complained grimly.

'You want me to go into business?' Kerry wished there was a seat somewhere around. Her legs were wobbly. She was afraid there was a catch, and this was some gigantic misunderstanding.

'That was the idea, but . . . '

'I knew there was a but.'

'The baby,' Alex reproved and spread his expressive hands wide. 'I didn't know there was going to be a baby. Do you think you could wait until after its birth to start this place up? I am afraid it would be too taxing a project to begin now, but when the baby is born we can get a nanny . . . '

She sagged. The but had not contained the tripwire she feared. Silence fell. She was in the trancelike hold of astonishment. Alex had opened the door of her gilded cage.

He expelled his breath. 'I know you like to be busy. You have so much energy. When the house is finished, Nicky at school, what would you do with yourself? I suggest you hire a manager so that you are not too tied to the business, but that is up to you.'

She wanted to cry. When Athene heard about this, she would think her son had gone crazy. 'You thought about this in Greece?'

'I know how bored you were before at home. You needed more stimulus. This time I want you to be content in our marriage, and here you will have your own challenge, you will . . .'

'Alex, it's the most wonderful thing anybody's ever done for me!' she interrupted extravagantly. In buying her this business, Alex had overcome his need to lock her up. She could see in his dark, set features that he was still questioning his own decision and was somewhat ambivalent about his own generosity. But what mattered was that he had done it for her despite his own fear of giving her this amount of freedom. She reached for his hand uncertainly. 'You won't ever have cause to regret this.'

His ebony brows pleated. 'I have to trust you. You were right when you said that. The problem was mine,' he stated tautly. 'That day on the island, I shocked myself. It will never happen again. I promise you that.'

Her bronze lashes veiled her stinging eyes. How like Alex it was to force himself into the very opposite of what he wanted when he realised that he was behaving unreasonably. She could have applauded his determination on a much less extreme show of trust than this, and suddenly she could see hope for them both, without Vickie or Jeff. Surely it was possible that, when Alex had dealt with his own gremlins, he would come back to her in every way?

Five days later, Alex flew to Rome. He was due

home for the weekend, but the afternoon passed without his appearance. Early evening, Kerry was perched on the window seat in the salon, wondering why he hadn't phoned, when a little yellow Fiat came bowling noisily down the driveway. A tall blond man extracted himself awkwardly from the driver's side and straightened. Vickie strolled round the bonnet and grasped his hand. Kerry froze. They had actually come. A minute later, Lucrezia showed them in.

'Alex is in Rome, he isn't back yet,' was the first thing Kerry said.

In the uneasy stasis, Jeff stuck out his hand, a dull flush of red lying along his broad cheekbones, his other arm planted round her strained sister. 'I don't expect you to like me, but I'm four years older and wiser now,' he said wryly.

'I guess you've been wondering what was going on,' Vickie said very quietly. 'Jeff never knew that you and Alex split up that day. I don't want you to feel he's equally to blame. It was over two years before we ran into each other again. I started seeing Jeff, but I had to keep quiet about it. I couldn't take him home, I couldn't tell you about him. It was poetic justice, I suppose. I was caught in my own trap.'

'I had absolutely no idea why Vickie was holding me at bay. If I had done, believe me, I wouldn't have let it lie,' he stressed levelly.

'The day you left me . . . I was upset,' Vickie muttered. 'I phoned Jeff and I told him everything.'

'And I flew off half-cocked to Athens, without really thinking the whole thing through. Your reaction when I called made me appreciate that it was going to take more than a few words,' Jeff admitted.

Vickie took a seat stiffly, still watching Kerry's anxious face. 'As you've probably guessed, I refused

to come initially. I'm not proud of that. It was unforgivable. I don't win any badges for courage. I
couldn't have done it without Jeff's support. I did love
Alex, Kerry,' she faltered and looked up at the man by
her side. 'But never the way I love Jeff. I'm glad it's
over, you have no idea what a relief it is . . . '

Jeff cleared his throat impatiently. 'I think right
now Kerry has to be more interested in hearing that
we've seen Alex.'

'You've seen him,' Kerry echoed. 'But how?'

'I thought it would be wiser if we saw your husband
at his office, and didn't involve you until we saw how
it was going to go,' Jeff supplied.

Kerry shut her eyes, rocked off balance to learn that
the deed had already been done. 'What did he say?'

'It was . . . ghastly,' her sister said shakily. 'He went
all quiet. It was like the whole thing just suddenly
sunk in on him. One minute he was raging, the next
he sat down.'

'But did he believe you?' Kerry pressed in
exasperation.

Jeff drove his fingers through his untidy hair ruefully.
'Oh, I think he believed us all right. I'm not sure he
would have if we hadn't both been there, though.'

'You said he went quiet? Pleased quiet? Angry
quiet?' Kerry prompted in desperation.

'He was appalled . . . stunned,' Vickie answered
reluctantly.

'But he hasn't come home.'

'He does have a lot to think about.' Her sister
looked at her guiltily, unhappily. 'He divorced you.
Finding out the truth now, when it's too late to really
do anything about it . . . ' Vickie hesitated. 'You see, I
never thought about how it was going to be for him.
Telling him the truth wasn't really giving him any-

thing to celebrate. That's the best way I could put it . . . '

Kerry viewed her in blank incomprehension. Alex ought to have been jetting home in haste to . . . to what? Fling himself at her feet and apologise? Like Vickie, she had never thought beyond the moment when Alex would know the true story. She had never questioned how Alex might react.

'I think it's time we left,' Jeff said bluntly. 'We're booked into a hotel, and the last thing Alex needs is to find us plonked here when he does come back.'

'Do you think if we held off getting married for a few months, you and Alex would come?' Vickie whispered uncertainly.

'Frankly, I think your sister has got more on her mind right now.' Jeff's tone was dry and Vickie reddened.

Kerry gave way to her sister's red-rimmed eyes and gave her a brief hug. The ice was broken, but she still could not have looked Vickie in the eye and told her that she completely forgave her. The cost had been too high. She managed to smile as she saw them off. It was difficult. Alex's delayed return was worrying her increasingly. She phoned the family house in Rome to speak to Mario, who was presently working as one of Alex's aides. She learnt that Alex had left the office before lunch time. By the time she got off the phone, she regretted calling. Athene had come on to the line to ask if there was anything wrong.

At two in the morning, she finally went to bed, and anxiety had been replaced by anger. How could he do this to her? Didn't he realise how worried she would be?

CHAPTER TEN

IT WAS noon the next day before Alex arrived home. He was as sleek and immaculate as ever, but he looked as if he had been up all night. Aside from the faint pallor, the etching of strain round his mouth, Kerry could not have read a single emotion in his shuttered dark gaze. He stared at her and sank down on to a sofa. For a moment his glossy head was bent, and then he lifted it again and the air of vulnerability was gone.

'I should have phoned, but I should imagine that is the least of my sins,' he began.

'Vickie and Jeff came here last night. I know you've seen them,' she interposed.

A wintry smile firmed his mouth. 'I almost made a derogatory comment about them both, but you have a saying about people in glass houses . . . ' He paused, his bone structure prominent beneath his bronze skin. 'I spent the night in the car. I didn't know what to say to you then. I needed time. Your sister informed me that she had told you the truth before you married me. Why didn't you tell me?'

The impatience had drained out of her. A curious foreboding was clenching her tight now. 'I didn't think you'd believe me.'

He bit out a harsh laugh and studied his linked hands. 'You know me too well. I shouldn't have asked the question. A more caring and less intimidating husband might have invited confidence. I don't blame you for keeping quiet. Jeff . . . it was he who phoned you on the island? You were very happy that day,' he drawled in the same measured, carefully unemotional tone.

'Of course I was . . . after all this time, I finally saw a hope of it all being cleared up,' she replied.

'It is now.' Releasing his breath slowly, he stared across the room at her. 'An apology, no matter how deeply it was meant, would be another insult to the many I have already offered you. In my desire for revenge, I have done you incalculable harm. Nothing I could do or say would make up for the pain I have caused you.'

Her eyes were haunted pools in the ashen pallor of her face. Her fingers curled tightly over the back of the armchair in front of her. She felt sick because she was afraid. If he loved her, there was plenty he could do, but he did not love her. Faced with his own mistrust and misjudgement, all Alex could feel now was the heavy burden on his conscience, the impossibility of finding adequate words to express his regret for all that had happened between them since that day in Venice.

'You said that the clock could not work in reverse,' he reminded her. 'You were correct. Even before they came to see me yesterday I had already seen this. I had also come to appreciate that a . . . loving husband would not have behaved as I did four years ago. I might have seen that if my wife did end up in another man's arms, my own behaviour had undoubtedly contributed to the betrayal. But then I was not capable of seeing that . . . '

'Alex . . . I . . . ' she faltered, torn by his pain but held back by his icy control.

He rose abruptly to his feet and moved a silencing hand. 'No, don't tell me not to say these things. I must say them. I fell in love with you because you were so full of life, and then I proceeded to crush it out of you,' he breathed contemptuously. 'Worse,' he continued before she could argue that his faults had not been so severe. 'I didn't even notice I was doing that to you.'

Her fingernails bit into the velvet beneath her hand. 'It wasn't so bad as that,' she protested weakly.

The dark head flung back. 'Do not be so generous to me,' he grated. 'When was I ever generous to you? Had I left you in the life you were contented with, I would feel less like some Dark Ages tyrant now. But no, once again I had to come into your life and make a mess of it, even to the point of making you pregnant again. And why did that happen? Because I blackmailed you into bed. I might as well have raped you.'

Kerry was trembling. So much of the understanding she had once longed for had been locked up inside him. It must have existed before yesterday. Alex could not have put all this together overnight. But what she was hearing was too extreme, too terrifyingly linked with a hard, bitter finality for her to receive any comfort from it.

He drew something from his inside pocket. 'This is the contract I forced you to sign.' He tore the document violently in half and cast the pieces into the grate. He straightened again, pale but controlled. 'Now you have no restrictions. I will leave you to lead your life as you choose to lead it. If you do not want me to see Nicky,' his voice roughened and dropped low, 'this I will accept, too.'

Shock was coursing through her in waves. Dear God, it was happening all over again! Only this time he had had the decency not to send a lawyer to do the dirty work. A searing memory of the letters she had written and the calls she had once made sealed her lips rigidly on any protest. If he was leaving, she would let him leave. Why should she tell him that she loved him, when her feelings weren't returned? She refused to make the smallest move to argue his decision.

'You married me just to get revenge, didn't you?' she accused with stark eyes. 'And once you'd got it, it was worthless, wasn't it?'

His dark eyes flamed golden. 'Yes . . . worthless,' His low-pitched response was wry. 'And I know that to give you your freedom back when it should never have been taken from you is poor recompense. But it is all that I have to give.'

All that he had to give. The statement rippled through her slight body, burning and wounding wherever it touched. It took her anger away. It numbed her. 'And what am I supposed to do now?' she asked woodenly.

'You do whatever you want. I will do nothing. You can have a divorce, a separation, whatever you choose. Where you live is also your decision,' he laid out tautly. 'Naturally, I will leave this house . . . '

'That's very generous of you, but I can be generous too,' she assured him shakily. 'I'll pack for you!'

'I have already asked Lucrezia to take care of it,' Alex murmured tightly. 'This is what you want, isn't it?'

'Of course it's what I want. My God, Alex, you don't think I'm about to argue, do you?' she gibed, half an octave higher.

A tiny muscle jerked at the corner of his compressed mouth, as if her venom had thrust fully home. In a torment of blind rage and despair, she watched him leave the room. She listened to his steps ringing up the stairs, and it seemed no time until they came down again. Still she had not moved. The slam of a car door echoed through the window. Unexpectedly, the door opened again.

Alex hovered there, shorn of his usual cool poise. But then, the last time he had walked out, he had not had to tolerate an audience or a conscience. She observed him with cold eyes. 'Did you forget something?'

Alex, you bastard, how could you put me through this again? But she didn't speak. As he turned on his heel, she crammed a shaking hand to her wobbling mouth and bowed her head over the chair which was still supporting her. Why was it that no matter what she did he could still walk away? Here she had been, expecting at first guilty discomfiture upon his part but inevitably the same release she had experienced after Vickie's revelations. But the one salient fact she had overlooked was that Alex did not love her. Alex had reacted according to his principles. He had forced her into this marriage. In apology, he was removing himself from her life again. She was fiercely glad that she had let him go thinking that she was delighted to see the back of him. Once before, loving him had humiliated her. It had not done so this time.

A quiet like the grave settled over Casa del Fiore. The staff seemed to creep about. Lucrezia, full of enormous Florentine compassion, looked upon her with great, tragic eyes and endeavoured to tempt her flagging appetite. At the end of a week, Kerry was emptied of tears. Her misery had stirred Nicky into rampant insecurity, and she had to pull herself together for his benefit. After the strain of smiling all day, she ended up ringing Steven late one evening. It was a long call, and forty-eight hours later Steven arrived on the doorstep.

Nicky greeted him boisterously and, under

Lucrezia's dazed scrutiny, Kerry threw her arms about his too. 'That'll have to be some shoulder,' she sniffed.

His classic features pulled a clownish grimace, and his blue eyes were rueful. 'It's one of the very few things I'm good

'Why didn't you tell him how you felt?' he asked later, when Nicky was in bed.

'There was no point.' Her tone brooked no argument.

'I've never met Alex . . . '

'Aren't you the lucky one?' she muttered, blowing her nose. 'He was a jealous, suspicious toad the first time around, but you know, this time he was worse . . . he was so nice all the time, it was like living with a saint over the last few weeks. Not my idea of Alex at all.'

Steven looked understandably a little at sea, and tried to be constructive. 'My gut reaction is that in clearing out he thought he was doing the decent thing, like somebody out of one of those ghastly melodramatic plays they enjoy in Greece.'

Kerry was unimpressed. 'If he hadn't wanted to let me go, he wouldn't have. Let's talk about something more cheerful. He's gone and that's it, and I never, ever want to see him again. Do you hear me?' She snatched at another tissue and wiped at her overflowing eyes.

Steven stayed only for three days, and mentioned that he would be selling up the business. Barbara had convinced him that he would cope much better with a simple workshop in a town where there would be more demand for his services, and she was thinking of looking for a job closer to home. Kerry had to quell the unpleasant feeling that everybody else's problems were working out, while her own simply increased in complexity.

She let the workmen back into the house. Her life wasn't going to fall apart again, she assured herself. She had got by without Alex before, she would do so again. She kept herself busy and she fell into bed every night exhausted. Alex had been gone exactly three weeks when Athene arrived without so much as a polite call to advertise her intent.

Kerry, surprised with a scarf round her head, wearing a pair of jogging pants and a stripy rugby shirt Alex had once worn, stiffened as Athene strolled in, her cool, dark appraisal sweeping her in obvious recoil. 'Perhaps I should have warned you that I was coming.'

Kerry showed her into the small sitting-room, since the salon was being redecorated. Athene shed her coat and inched off her gloves. 'If it is not too impertinent a question, may I ask who the young man was that you had staying?'

Off-balance, Kerry stared back at her.

Athene quirked a silvery brow. 'Your housekeeper is related to one of my servants. Such news travels fast,' she remarked drily.

Kerry reddened. Athene in this formidable mood could only be compared to the iceberg which sank the Titanic. She found herself hurriedly making an explanation, and alluding carefully to Barbara's existence in Steven's life.

Athene's Arctic cool melted slightly. 'Ah,' she nodded. 'This makes greater sense. You don't look to be thriving upon my son's absence.'

'That's a matter of opinion,' Kerry parried proudly.

'I am not quite in my dotage,' Athene fielded, and her thin lips almost smiled. 'This outfit you wear can only be an expression of grief.' She paused and then looked up. 'I did not come here easily. You and I have only Alex in common, and I have come for Alex's sake.'

'Alex left me . . . ' Kerry began spiritedly.

Athene waved an imperious hand. 'But not, I think, willingly, and I have no need to receive details. I knew from the first moment I met you six years ago that you and Alex would have a stormy relationship. Given your personality, it was only a matter of time until the trouble began . . . '

'*My* personality?'

Athene frowned irritably. 'You are too defensive. Will you let me speak?' she demanded thinly. 'If Alex had married a quieter girl, content to fit with his expectations, the marriage probably would have lasted as yours did not. You were outgoing and lively, and Alex was stifling you because he could not bring himself to trust you. The fault was his. Perhaps I could have stopped it then by speaking to him. I chose to conserve my own dignity. I did not interfere, and when I would have done, it was too late.'

Kerry sighed. 'I'm afraid I don't see what you could have done.'

Athene smiled grimly. 'Yes, you have noticed that Alex and I are not close. Did you ever wonder why? Alex was my firstborn and my favourite, but I believe his first loyalty always lay with his father. Nevertheless, when he was a child, we were close until a certain episode occurred.' Her voice was becoming taut and hesitant. 'I lost my son's respect. Has he told you of this?'

Puzzled by the increasingly personal tenor of Athene's words, while marvelling that Athene could ever have done anything to fall foul of Alex's high principles, Kerry murmured gently, 'Alex wouldn't have told me anything of that nature unless there was a need for me to know.'

Athene sighed. 'It was not a need he would have acknowledged, and it is an episode he has done his utmost to forget. That I have always been aware of,' she conceded, almost as if she was talking to herself. 'When I married Alex's father, Lorenzo, I admired him very much. I was only a teenager when I understood that it was my parents' dearest wish that I should marry the son of their oldest friends. It was not arranged, you understand, but it was expected.'

'Were you unhappy with Alex's father?' Kerry prompted in surprise.

'When I fell in love, for the first and last time in my life,' Athene stressed looking her almost defiantly in the eye, 'then I was unhappy.'

As Kerry's face tightened in astonished realisation that Athene was admitting to having loved another man, her companion's lips compressed tightly.

'Why not me? None of us are born saints. I had been content with Lorenzo. He was a good man and a faithful husband, and he still loved me on the day he died. He never knew that for a few short weeks of our marriage I carried on an affair with another man, and it would have caused him great pain to discover that secret. He had always awarded me unquestioning faith and trust,' she admitted heavily.

Mottled colour had suffused her powdered cheeks, making Kerry sharply aware that this confession of frailty had cost Athene dearly.

'We met quite by accident,' she continued expressionlessly. 'He was a businessman, but not wealthy. For me, it was a kind of madness. I counted no costs when I became involved with him. Every moment I could steal from my family, I was with Tomaso, and inevitably we were found out.' Her voice had sunk very low. 'I wanted desperately to be with him somewhere where we could be alone. We used to have a summer place outside Cannes. Alex was at boarding-school then. He was to spend his half-term there with me. There was illness in the school and they let him leave early. He crept into the house to surprise me, and he discovered me in Tomaso's arms. He was only thirteen, and I was terrified that he would tell his father. I realised too late what I had done. I sent Tomaso away and I never saw him again. I had my children and my husband to consider. Alex remained silent. He understood that nothing could be gained from any other course but his father's pain and disillusionment.'

As the implications of the sad, reluctantly advanced confession swept Kerry in a stormy flood, she swallowed hard sooner than betray a sympathy which would be fiercely rejected. Athene might have strayed in the madness she described, but for a strong woman of deep, religious convictions her choice had been completely in character.

In the heavy silence, Athene took a deep breath. 'He didn't betray me, but I lost the son who loved and respected his mother that day. He never alluded to the incident again. How else could he behave?' she appealed tiredly. 'His love for his father tied him to silence. He grew up that day all at once. He learnt that appearances could be deceptive. Now perhaps you may understand why Alex would find it very hard to trust a woman.'

And why he divorced me and why he wouldn't come near me, Kerry added in inner anguish. He had been afraid to end up in the weak position he probably believed his father had held throughout his marriage. He had cut her out of his life sooner than risk that danger. 'Why have you told me this?' she asked.

'For Alex. The settlement of a debt,' Athene emphasised, looking every year of her age. 'Now perhaps you will go to him and tell him that there is no other man in your life.'

The edge of her contempt stiffened Kerry. 'It's not as simple as that. Alex doesn't love me.'

'Does that matter, if he needs you?' Athene turned on her like a lioness defending a cub. 'If there was a cure for you I would have given it to him! You are Alex's one weakness. I don't know how he kept away from you for four years. And you say, "he doesn't love me",' she mimicked in a die-away echo, but her lined dark eyes were suspiciously bright. 'Do you think I came here easily to ask for your help? He is on the island, and when I saw him last week he was exceedingly drunk. While you are painting your walls, my son is going to pieces!'

As Athene stalked back out to her car in high dudgeon, Kerry was picturing Alex standing in the doorway as he had that last day. Alex without words, simply taking a last look at her. Does it matter what drives him if he needs you? 'You can never be here for me when I need you.' The ragged condemnation he had uttered weeks ago thickened her throat. It was three steps to the phone, and she got there in one. If there was something wrong with Alex, she would go to him. Just once more she would put her own pride on the line. Athene would not have approached her lightly.

By the time she lurched out of the helicopter late that evening, and the pilot tucked Nicky's limp, sleeping body into her arms, her adrenalin-charged rush to Alex's side seemed a little excessive. Nobody was expecting them. Kerry had purposely not phoned. She had not wanted Alex to have time to prepare himself for her arrival.

Sofia hurried towards her in a dressing-gown, with Spiros in her wake. Kerry settled Nicky into the manservant's arms with a relieved sigh. She had been prepared for Alex to appear, looking his usual smooth self and embarrassingly curious about her uninvited descent. But he didn't appear, and Sofia fussed round her, trying to persuade her to go to bed. A thin bar of light was burning below the study door. Seeing it, Kerry turned from Sofia and opened the door.

The shutters were drawn, the air rank with the pervasive fumes of whisky. Alex was slumped in a chair, and she no longer needed to wonder why he had failed to come and greet her. He hadn't had a shave in days. He was haggard, his cheekbones protruding sharply to emphasise his unhealthy pallor. Her sleek, beautiful Alex had gone skinny, and he was viewing her with unfocused dark eyes much as a drunk uncritically accepts the presence of a parade of pink elephants.

'Oh . . . Alex, how could you do this to yourself?' she whispered painfully.

She threw open the shutters and the windows to let in fresh air. Something crunched under her shoe. She bent to lift a crumpled black and white photo of herself, a stolen photo taken when she was unwares some time in the past. She was emerging from the showroom, talking animatedly to Steven.

Alex muttered something incoherent. He closed his eyes and opened them again. 'Kerry?' he slurred uncertainly. 'Don't go away again.'

He pulled himself up in the chair and she stood over him with folded arms. 'Do you love me?' she demanded shakily, surmising that she was most likely to receive the truth in the condition he was in, and if she was taking advantage, too bad.

'You'll disappear if I say yes,' he mumbled accusingly.

'No, I won't. You've got that the wrong way round,' she protested.

He pushed unsteady fingers through his tousled black hair. 'Yes.'

Her eyes watered. 'Say it, then.'

His mouth curved into a shadowy smile, the sort of smile a pink elephant might inspire. 'I love you,' he managed, and then, 'Much too much to hold on to you.'

'No . . . no!' She could have kicked him. 'I didn't want the qualification. That's just so typical of you, Alex. You can't even say three little words the way I want to hear them. I've waited six years, and in six years I got it thrown at me in the past tense once, and now I get it with a qualification. If I had any pride at all, I wouldn't be here ready to tell you that *I* love *you* . . . '

She retreated, shocked by her own loss of control. But Alex had finally been sprung from his lethargy. He stood up, swaying slightly. 'Hallucinations don't shout.'

'I didn't mean to shout,' she answered shakily.

His hand lifted to touch a strand of her gleaming hair. 'I'm not fussy,' he muttered hoarsely. 'Did you mean it?'

'Yes.' She watched him breathe again, watched a gleam of vitality spark in his dulled eyes.

'And I have to be drunk.' Red washed his sallow complexion. He backed towards the door. 'I need a shower . . . I need a coffee. Don't go away.'

She wiped her eyes as he left the room. She had seen in his face what no counterfeiter could have copied.

The same pain, the same fear, the same loneliness, and she was ridiculously tempted to sit down and have a good cry. If he had left her, it had not been because he wanted to leave her. It was almost an hour before he reappeared. Either a miracle potion or simple shock had sobered him up. Shaven, his long, straight legs encased in tight jeans matched to a clean white shirt, he looked like Alex again, only not quite so confident as was his wont. He strode out of the bathroom impatiently, and then wheeled round in surprise to find her seated on the end of his bed.

'I thought you'd got lost,' she said, hot-cheeked.

'And I thought you were with Steven,' he drawled tautly.

She told him quietly what she had told Athene earlier in the day.

'He cares for someone else? How is this possible?'

'They've known each other since they were teenagers, and sometimes they don't see each other for months on end. He's a friend,' she hesitated, 'I wouldn't have been attracted to him in any other way, in any case; he can be a real pain . . . '

His strained mouth curved helplessly with humour. 'A pain . . . all I saw were those golden looks of his . . . for months.' His smile ebbed with discomfiture.

'I saw that photo. You must have spied on me. Why?'

'Is there always a sane explanation for the things we do?' he countered tautly. 'I told myself that I had a right to know what you were doing when you had my son. But when you began to go out socially with Steven, I couldn't bear it and who knows what goes on behind closed doors? I was afraid you might marry him. Then, when I saw you again, everything I had spent years denying came alive again. For a few days, I was like a man possessed. I didn't care what I had to do to get you back, I didn't even ask myself why I was doing it.'

A tender smile softened her lips. 'You're forgiven. If you hadn't used pressure, we wouldn't be here together now.'

The topaz eyes narrowed. 'How can you say that? *Per Dio* . . . I behaved like the savage you said I was.'

'I love you, Alex.'

He moved closer, his dark features clenched taut. 'I realised that I still loved you the first time we made love again, but I believed that you cared for Steven. At best you seemed to tolerate me, and then after that incident on the beach, you were cold in my arms. I had even killed that,' he emphasised with hard self-derision.

'I was upset, frightened by your jealousy,' she argued warily, wondering why he had yet to put his arms around her.

'I know.' In shamed acknowledgement, he looked at her guiltily. 'But I still could not have let you go. I couldn't face losing you. In the end, I was even relieved that you were pregnant. It was another way of holding on to you. It didn't matter that I couldn't make love to you any more, it didn't matter to me that you cared, as I thought, for another man. I still had you, and that was sufficient. When they came to me and told me the truth, everything came apart . . . ' His hand sketched a movement of defeat. 'Before, I believed I had rights, and I made excuses for myself. When I couldn't any more, all I could do was let you go, and it was hardly enough in the circumstances.'

Her patience was wearing thin. Did he plan to stand here for the rest of the night, unsmilingly endeavouring to persuade her that he was an undeserving cause? She could have walked on water after seeing the love in Alex when he was too low to work at concealment. Now she did something far less dangerous. She closed the distance he was carefully maintaining from her. Her hands cupped his hard cheekbones, her green eyes clinging to his. 'I didn't want to be let go. I love you. But I wasn't going to beg you to stay.'

The dark gaze positively shimmered. 'But . . . '

'No buts.' Her fingertip brushed his tense lower lip softly.

He searched her face torturously and then, with a groan, he locked her tightly to him. He trembled against her, and Kerry hugged him close as he buried his face in her hair, his voice muffled and gruff. 'Do you know what it was like to have to leave you? I hope you know what you are doing now. I could not leave again.'

For a long time he kept her imprisoned in his arms, and when he moved it was to back her down on to the bed with a husky sigh about the convenience of the setting she had chosen. 'I should tell you something,' he confided then, abruptly. 'There has never been another woman.'

Her lashes flew up in bemusement. 'I don't think I . . . '

His dark visage split with sudden amusement, the momentary and rare embarrassment she had seen there dissipating. 'I had this . . . er . . . complication.' His fingers toyed with the buttons on her blouse as he loosed them one by one. 'Every time I got that close to a woman, I would always think of you, and the desire

. . . it would recede. Didn't you notice how desperate I was that night in London? Four years is a very long time to feel that you are only half a man because you do not want to admit that you are still in love with your ex-wife.'

A slow and beatific smile was building on her lips.

Alex grinned. 'It was not very funny.'

'Serves you right.' Her hand roamed possessively over the hard thrust of his thighs evident beneath the tight jeans. As she realised what she was doing, she blushed, and his golden eyes clung to her adoringly.

'Yes, it served me right.' He rolled her back into his embrace. 'But I wasn't sorry when I got you back. We always belonged only to each other. I need very badly to remind myself of that now,' he whispered raggedly, and branded her mouth with the fever of the fierce, raw hunger that spoke for itself.

'What made you come to me?' he prompted when she was still languorous with the exquisite release of their lovemaking.

She hid her expression against his shoulder, and her arms tightened convulsively round him. 'Athene visited me.'

He tensed, his dark, dishevelled head lifting up.

'Yes,' she confirmed. 'She told me, and it hurt her to tell me. She loves you very much, Alex.'

His breath escaped in a hiss. 'She didn't love my father, did she admit that? He adored her. I could never bear to watch him dance attention on her after that day. I was afraid ever to be like that with a woman . . . yes, it influenced me when we were first married, how could it not? I could never accept that you could love me as I loved you,' he completed roughly.

'But I do,' she stressed, smoothing his cheek gently. 'And loving me isn't a weakness, Alex.'

Hard fingers caught her chin, a rueful smile slanting his lips. 'But I am weak with you. My life is hell without you; how could it be otherwise? All those years wasted because I was too proud to come to you . . . what a bloody fool I was!' he swore fiercely. 'Nothing was worth what we both went through apart. So much unhappiness, so many mistakes.'

Her heart leapt in her throat as he looked at her. The dark-fringed golden eyes were unguarded, nakedly vulnerable for a split second as he wrapped her firmly against him again. 'But this time I will love you always, no matter what the future brings. Perhaps I will never have the words to express how much you mean to me,' he sighed regretfully.

'I don't know. Superhusband wasn't doing too badly on actions,' she teased. 'I was very slow on the uptake.'

'Super . . . husband?' Alex growled.

She grinned. 'All that boundless bonhomie . . . '

A reflective smile removed his frown. 'It wasn't easy. I was hoping to convert you from Steven. But patience . . . it is not my strong point. I don't know how I kept my hands from you; it was a torture to do so.' The husky confession was feelingly reminiscent of the deprivation he had endured, and already his natural assurance was reasserting its sway. 'Never again.'

She rested back invitingly. 'I second that.'

'Why is it that you always have the last word?' But he won silence by his own nefarious means, and laughter shook her slightly before she gave herself up, without a care in the world, to Alex's mastery.

Harlequin Presents

Coming Next Month

Available in June wherever paperback books are sold, or through
Harlequin Reader Service:

In the U.S.
901 Fuhrmann Blvd.
P.O. Box 1397
Buffalo, N.Y. 14240-1397

In Canada
P.O. Box 603
Fort Erie, Ontario
L2A 5X3

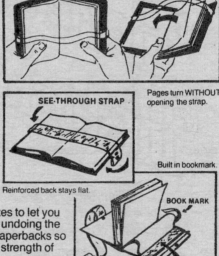